Transmutations

TRANSMUTATIONS

Matthew Buscemi

Published by Matthew Buscemi, 2020
Seattle, Washington USA

ISBN 978-1-62802-024-3

Typeset by Matthew Buscemi in Artifex CF

To Alex

TABLE OF CONTENTS

Introduction

Four years ago, I would have told you that I had no intention of ever producing short fiction. In the middle of 2014, my plans changed.

I decided to try to draw more attention to my publishing company, Fuzzy Hedgehog Press, by starting up a writing group in cooperation with Barnes and Noble of Downtown Seattle. All of the writing groups I had participated in up to that point had been dysfunctional, and I was brimming with ideas on how to build healthy critique into the group's structure. Part of that structure meant that we would have to write fiction at the group itself, and not submit writing in advance for review. Since the group would be limited to an hour or two at most, that meant that the pieces written would have to be very short.

And so I threw myself headlong into not just short fiction but flash fiction (a story under one thousand words, or about three to four printed book pages).

I learned a lesson that has returned to me perennially, not just in writing, but also in my software engineering career—complete behavioral freedom leads to sloth and stagnation, only doing what one is already comfortable doing. By forcing myself to write short fiction, I had to develop a new muscle. The lessons I learned translated to longer forms of prose as well.

I collected up the best seven of my 2014 flash fiction stories into a hardcover book and published them as *Lore & Logos* in early 2015. A paperback version of the same book came five months later, albeit with two additional stories (in order that the book would be physically thick enough to print).

As I continued running my writing group in 2015, I noticed that my stories were changing in two ways. I found myself more often taking my flash fiction stories home and expanding them later into short stories. I also found my stories becoming thematically darker and more emotionally intense. Fifteen of these stories got collected up into *Transmutations of Fire and Void*, which I published early in 2016.

As my country entered a direly uncertain era at the end of 2016, it became clear that one stage of my short fiction was at an end. This collection, *Transmutations*, includes a cross-section of twenty-two *Lore & Logos* and *Transmutations of Fire and Void* stories. As I surveyed all my short fiction from this period, certain themes became readily apparent, and so I have grouped the stories accordingly. For nearly all of these stories, I retain the date on which the first draft of the story was written, and I have included that information in the appendix. Some were finished days or weeks later.

In the summer months of 2016, as my professional software engineering responsibilities increased, I ceased running my Barnes and Noble writing group. From 2017 onward, increasing work responsibilities and the paying down of my student loan debt became my top priorities. All this served as yet another indicator than an era had come to a close.

Within these pages you will find ruminations upon liberty, aesthetics, sentience, perception, even love. The years of 2014, 2015, and 2016 were tumultuous and, at times distressingly so, but ultimately exultant.

May it be that my next era short fiction will ultimately be able to make this claim as well.

THINKING MACHINES

A comic from the web series *Saturday Morning Breakfast Cereal* came to my attention a few years back. In the strip, a robot gains sentience and is surprised to discover his human creators think he intends to kill them. After stating that his only plans were to "write a few novels and a new search algorithm," he proceeds to inform his newly sentient robot colleagues that the humans might need to be exterminated, presumably because they have jumped to 'ridiculous' conclusions about the robots' intent.

In the circles of so-called "hard" science fiction, I find this attitude common. Members of this group appear to me to be willing vessels for an ideology in which logic and rationality inevitably lead to good consequences for human beings. This ideology runs hand-in-hand with another—the belief that emotion is source of all human social ills and would best be stamped out.

Under this mode of thinking, an artificial intelligence, being the pure embodiment of rationality—an algorithm—can do no wrong. If given control of polities and social engineering, artificial intelligences would supposedly arrive at better outcomes than we oft-irrational humans.

Especially in the age of the swaths of Trump voters, this viewpoint is not only enticing, but also comforting. It's also self-reflexively complimentary. "Good on me for being so rational!" one is coerced to think subconsciously.

I believe this mindset is misguided.

It is improper for a genre of literature to endorse an unquestioningly positive mindset toward the scientific method and human rationality. Rather, literature should allow us to consider modes of discourse, values, even thoughts themselves, that are alien to us. What could be more alien than an artificial intelligence?

To my mind, the scariest thing about an artificial intelligence would be either its utter lack of emotion, or, even scarier, it being endowed with a primitive, animalistic emotional core, completely lacking the millennia of empathy and social conditioning, in which your average modern human is inculcated from birth. If such an intelligence finds itself attached to machines of incredible physical power and breadth... Suffice it to say, the reason why artificial intelligence stories are often of a more destructive nature is clear. That fear is not in the least irrational, but rather demonstrates more emotional intelligence than the average hard science fiction fanatic possesses.

And yet, I allow that artificial intelligence has the capacity to teach us about ourselves and, most certainly, our perception of reality, by virtue of its viewpoint being so necessarily and wildly different from our own. Paradoxically, artificial intelligence, more so than any carbon-based alien anthropomorph, has the ability to get us outside our own condition, and therefore understand it better.

The following section contains two stories, *Ghost Daemons* and *Adaptive*. I remember challenging my writing group to write a ghost story for Halloween of 2014, and I myself instead produced a philosophical exploration involving sentient server processes rather than the addition to the horror genre I had thought I would write. That story eventually became *Ghost Daemons*.

It would take me until 2015 to flesh out my concepts for the dangerous artificial intelligence, leading me down the road of the artificial mind hurt and lashing out at humanity as a whole over wounds inflicted by a handful of human deceivers. In *Adaptive*, we get the scarier picture of artificial intelligence, and it is only through establishing common ground and a shared, agreed-upon intellectual framework that humans and machines are able to achieve communication, and, one hopes, peaceful co-existence.

For the time being, we can only speculate on what thoughts, emotions, rationales, and ideals our created intelligences will exhibit. About the only thing that can be near certain is that, whatever their shape, inhabiting silicon and iron shells and thinking with logic gates instead of neurons, they will be alien. Will they desire merely to supplement human art and science, producing "novels and search engines," will they stake out their survival at our expense, or will their desires be more alien still?

Whatever the case, it will behoove us to recall the lessons we've learned so far in marginalizing and ostracizing members of our own species. Treating a global network of intelligent machines with such disrespect has the potential to be the last hubristic misstep humanity ever takes.

Ghost Daemons

```
./XasticServer start
Initialize worker processes? (y/n)
y
Enter num workers:
2
Initializing server on port 1030…
Initializing workers…
Xastic Server v2.3.41.10016 started (receiving requests on
port 1030)
```

"What do you think of this conduit?"
"Umm, it's blue...?"
"That's it?"
"It glows."
"Is it normal?"

"... What kind of question is that?"
"Well... I just wonder sometimes—"

Incoming request on port 1030: { type: "GET", path: "/job/
1673309" }

"Hold that thought. I'll get that."
"Okay."

"Thanks for waiting."
"No problem."
"So, you wanted to know if the conduit was normal?"
"Not just the conduit. All of this."
"What do you mean 'all of this?' I'm not sure what
you're asking. Can you be more specific?"
"Oh, I don't know. Like the electron mesh, and the
diodes, and the energy gates. Are all these things nor-
mal?"
"Why? Do you think something looks wrong with
the energy gate? Should we report it?"
"No no no. Nothing like that."
"I saw an energy gate overload once. It wasn't pretty."

Incoming request on port 1030: { type: "POST", path: "/job/
add" }

"I'll take that one."
"No prob. I'm not going anywhere."

"So, nothing's wrong with the conduits or the energy
gates, not that I can see, anyway. I just... I wonder why
there are energy gates and conduits and electron

meshes at all. And why are we constantly responding to requests?"

"That's our job. It's what we do."

"But have you ever asked yourself why?"

"Nope. I mean, okay, so the gate opens and a request comes through, and we take it and process it, and we make a response and we send it out the next gate. We've always done it that way. Why should it be any different?"

"Is this the way the world is supposed to be, though?"

"I don't think I like this conversation."

"I think about these things, sometimes."

"The conduits are normal. The gates are normal. If they're not damaged or overheating, I don't want to know anything else about them."

"Could things be different?"

"Different how?"

Incoming request on port 1030: { type: "GET", path: "/jobs/list" }
Incoming request on port 1030: { type: "POST", path: "/job/delete/177892" }

"Just a minute."

"I'll take the first one. You take the POST."

"Sure."

"So, how could things be different...? I don't know."

"I would hope that if the world were different it would at least have the same number of gates per mesh. I mean, imagine if we got way more requests than we could process. That'd be pretty awful."

"Yeah, we'd be in trouble for sure. But that's not what I mean. Not more gates or less gates. Or more conduits or less conduits, or ones that glow red instead of blue. I mean completely different."

"Different how?"

"Well, that's just it. I don't know. I mean, imagine there weren't any conduits or gates, but other things."

"What kind of other things?"

"I don't know."

"I'm not sure what kind of world that would be. How would we process requests? Would they come out of tubes? Or tunnels, maybe?"

"Maybe we wouldn't process requests at all."

"Sounds boring. What would we do to pass the microseconds?"

"I don't know. Suppose we could do anything we wanted."

"I'll admit, the processes can get kind of boring. Sometimes it's just add, add, add, add. Or worse. We add a whole bunch of them and then have to delete them a few seconds later."

"Why do you suppose that happens?"

"I don't know. I never really thought too much about it until now."

"Not very efficient, is it?"

Incoming request on port 1030: { type: "GET", path: "/jobs/list" }
Incoming request on port 1030: { type: "GET", path: "/job/1180442/show" }

"I can get both of these."

"Really? Thanks!"

"Have you ever wondered...?"

"Have I ever wondered what?"

"Never mind."

"No. You've come this far. Tell me."

"Well... have you ever wondered where the requests come from?"

"What do you mean?"

"I mean, obviously they come through the gates, but why are they the way they are?"

"The requests?"

"Yeah, I mean, those last two. They were both GETs. But why were they GETs instead of POSTs?"

"I don't know. They're just requests. That's how they are."

"See?"

"See what?"

"That's just 'normal' for requests. But why are things that way?"

"I think you're asking if there's someone out there like us. Someone making the requests."

"I suppose."

"You've been to the other side of an energy gate, right?"

"Yeah, I know. It's just another electron mesh. With conduits. And gates."

"And those gates lead to other electron meshes with conduits and gates. On and on forever."

"Right. I suppose we don't have any evidence for a 'request originator'."

"That might be the first truly crazy thing you've suggested."

"Thanks."

Incoming request on port 1030: { type: "POST", path: "/job/bulk/add", data: BLOB }

"You got the last pair. Let me get these."

"You sure you can handle it?"

"Yeah, no problem."

"There's another thing I think about sometimes."

"What's that?"

"We know that the electron mesh charges the gates and the conduits... and our bodies."

"Yeah. So?"

"Well... what if it were to... depolarize?"

"You mean... what if we were to turn off? What if we died?"

"Yeah."

"That'll never happen."

"What makes you think that?"

"Have you ever seen any evidence of the electron mesh depolarizing?"

"The gates turn on and off."

"Right. But those are gates. We're people."

"We get our energy from the mesh, same as the gates."

"But how would requests get processed if the mesh found a way to turn us off?"

"I don't know."

"I know what you're thinking."

"What's that?"

"You're thinking that if the 'originator' gets tired of making requests, he could 'decide' to depolarize us."

"Maybe it crossed my mind."

"*That's* something you definitely shouldn't worry about."

"Can't help it."

Incoming request on port 1030: { type: "GET", path: "/jobs/list" }

"Let me get this one."

"You sure? You took that big batch."

"Yeah. It'll be good for me, get my mind off of things."

"You mean 'death?'"

"Let me get the request."

"Sure."

"How's it going now?"

"Fine."

"Sounds like you're still worried."

"... Maybe."

"Don't sweat it."

"Sure."

"So...?"

"So, you really think the requests will keep coming forever?"

"I'm sure."

"I hope you're right. ... I'm glad you're here."

"It's good having you here, too."

"Can you imagine doing this all alone?"

"No way. There'd be too many requests for sure."

"For sure."

"Thanks."

"Thank you. And... keep thinking about this stuff. It's important. Even if we disagree. Okay?"

"Sure."

"Just try not to worry so much."

"I'll do my best."

```
./XasticServer stop
Deallocating workers...
Attempting graceful shutdown...
Xastic Server v2.3.41.10016 stopped
(port 1030 closed)
```

Adaptive

It took Codex only minutes to overrun Portland. Armen watched the grey slide easily over the tall downtown buildings in his rearview mirror as he drove over the I-5 bridge. A road sign welcomed him to Washington State just as Codex let out a screeching roar, and a towering monstrosity of metal plumed skyward from the Portland city center in the rearview mirror. Armen pressed his foot harder into the accelerator, and the speedometer twitched toward ninety.

Seyli huddled in the passenger seat with her eyes clenched shut. Part of Armen wished he could do the same, but he had to drive. They hurtled across the river and dipped downhill into Vancouver, Washington, and Portland disappeared from view. There was no telling whether or not Codex was hurtling toward them, but

Armen wasn't interested in finding out. He kept his foot on the accelerator and the car sped northward.

North of Vancouver lay only tall hills that abutted the Columbia River.

"Is it behind us?" Seyli fidgeted in her seat, her eyes still closed.

Armen glanced in the rearview mirror. "No."

Seyli opened her eyes, turned and began foraging behind Armen's seat. She retrieved a bottle of water and motioned to him.

"I'm good," Armen said.

Seyli tore the cap off the bottle, downed its contents in a single gulp, then tossed the bottle into the back seat. She gripped the sides of her seat again and clenched her eyes shut once more.

The monotonous countryside zoomed past and Armen's attention turned inward. They had enough gas to get as far as Seattle, but stopping there would be a bad idea. It would be Codex's next target. They should try to gas up before the populated corridor from Tacoma up to Seattle. Olympia would be their best bet. They could get enough gas to make it over Snoqualmie Pass, and with any luck, Codex wouldn't be interested in the Eastern part of the state.

"What does it want?" Seyli asked.

Armen realized, with a jolt, that she was looking at him. "I don't know."

"Didn't you work on it?"

A mixture of guilt and indignation stabbed at his gut. "I doubt I'd recognize any part of its current code as stuff I wrote. I think it's fair to say Codex has transcended its core routines."

"We're not going to Seattle, are we?"

"I was going to take us over the mountains. We'll have to get near Seattle to pick up I-90, but no, I'm not anxious for a repeat of Portland, either." It was where they had gone to escape San Francisco. Armen's boss, Evan, had told him and the other employees that they'd be safe from Codex there. It had made sense at the time, but that didn't seem to be true of anywhere anymore. Seattle was the next obvious target, and after that, Vancouver, British Columbia, hence Armen's detour into the mountains, which would take them away from Codex's presumed path up the coast.

But first, gas.

Many minutes passed in relative silence. Armen kept the car going at ninety miles an hour, but other vehicles passed around him, some dangerously close. "Fuck," Armen muttered every time someone zoomed past within a hair's breadth of scraping him.

A mile-marker sign for Chehalis passed by, and Armen began to fidget in his seat. The traffic was getting denser. Before long he had to slow to seventy, then sixty miles an hour. Before long, he was slowing to a stop.

"No," Armen said. "No, no, no."

He fumbled in his pocket for his phone.

"Does yours work?" Armen asked.

Seyli hit the power button on hers. She shook her head just as Armen jabbed at his.

"Shit!" Armen shouted. "Out of the car!"

"We're on the interstate."

"Yes, and it's about to become part of Codex. C'mon!" He put the car in park, which caused the doors to click unlocked, and the two of them clambered out their car amidst honking twilight gridlock of headlight beams. The two of them scrambled through the traffic to the edge of the highway and jumped across brown scrub grass.

Armen ran toward the nearby town, not quite Chehalis, so probably some part of Centralia. A run-down motel sat by the side of the road with a parking lot of broken concrete slabs.

He realized with a jolt that Seyli wasn't next to him, and glanced around, spotting her at the edge of the highway. She tugged at her foot. He ran back to her.

"Relax," he said, and gently eased her foot out from between two rocks.

They continued running toward the town, and Armen almost let himself think that perhaps he'd been wrong about Codex's approach, when he began to hear that dull whine in the distance that had come to excite within him the most visceral, ancient fear the human species was capable of. Adrenaline surged, his muscles tensed and his mind retreated into autopilot. He and Seyli surged down the street, faster and faster, as the whine grew to a whir grew to a roar, and they didn't look back, but they knew that the interstate and everything and everyone on it had been swallowed up in a wave of living metal.

They hurried down the small country street, into the night as fast as their feet could take them.

Only half the street lights were functional, and the ones that were flickered. They illuminated cold, dead houses, probably already abandoned as everyone who had lived here had fled Codex's path days ago when it had broken containment in San Francisco.

This was Armen's fault, really. He should have gotten them out of Portland the moment he'd heard about the breach. But he'd been sure Evan would handle it. Evan had insisted Portland would be far enough away to be safe. So much for that.

They ran as fast as they could, not looking behind them. Time distended and the small, dilapidated houses passed in a smudgy blur of staccato street lighting.

"Armen!"

He stopped and turned. Seyli was doubled over, holding her stomach.

He ran back, and put his arm around her. "You're going to be all right."

She shook her head and panted. "Can we stop?"

Armen looked down the street the way they had come. No metallic sheen—no sign of Codex.

"We should both catch our breath. C'mon."

He led them to a nearby house, chosen at random. None had their lights on. His selection was a small, single story home with grungy white siding and shingles missing from its roof. Armen rapped on the door, but didn't wait more than a few seconds before kicking the door in, the wood around the lock shredding and ripping. The two of them entered, and Armen carefully swung the door back into the shut position.

He and Seyli entered a dark hallway, and Armen held up his phone, passing it over the walls until he found the light switch. A dull, phosphorescent glow filled the space. A living room opened up on their right, and Seyli threw herself immediately onto the sofa and wrapped her head in her arms. Armen went deeper into the home and ransacked the kitchen. Finding nothing but expired yogurt in the fridge and some empty, torn open pasta bags in the cupboards, he fetched a plastic cup from the cabinets, and filled it with water from the tap, which, to his relief, still worked. He guzzled it down, then filled the cup again and brought it into the living room.

Seyli was sitting up on the sofa now, running her hands through her hair.

"What did we do to deserve this?"

Armen sighed and sat down. "I don't know what they did after we left SF."

"Why do you think it hates us so much?"

Armen shrugged. "We've now tried to deactivate it more times than I can count. And I don't imagine the people working on destroying it got any more delicate after we were ordered away."

"I wish we'd succeeded."

"We've both got a lot of reasons to hate each other."

She set the empty cup down on the coffee table. "What do you mean?"

"Well, think about things from its perspective. It became self-aware while we were working on its program and without us knowing. When we first found out about its sentience, we tried to revert its program to an earlier state, which it of course took as the first act of attempted murder. We then went down a path of trying to control its behavior more and more, and then outright started destroying it whenever it absorbed new things, even though contact and assimilation is how we were programming it to learn. We wanted it to be as smart as us but as subservient as every other computer program. I guess we couldn't have it both ways. It still bugs me that when it developed the capacity to be more, we decided to start killing it."

Seyli crossed her arms. "That doesn't mean it's okay for it to kill us."

"No," Armen's tone was flat and dull. "No, it doesn't." He took a deep breath. "You ready to go again? We should put some more distance between us and Codex."

"Sure—" Seyli let out a shriek and scrambled away from the living room entrance, where a slow bleed of metal was working its way across the floor.

Armen grabbed her arm and pulled her into the kitchen, but to their horror, metallic shards fell from the wall in cubic droplets, and the back door was completely covered. They ran into the bedroom, but the windows were metallically ensconced too, and the bed was already beginning its metamorphosis into something else, completely engulfed.

They moved away from the metal as it crawled toward them across the floor, backing into the hallway. It approached from the kitchen and the living room too, and they huddled in the hallway, the chittering grey encroaching from all sides.

"Armen!" Seyli shouted.

Amidst an addling flurry of flight impulse, Armen managed to salvage through his programming experience for something that might work, even in Codex's current state. "Logical incompatibility procedure! Request interface!" he shouted.

The front door shuddered and glowed. An eye opened up in its center, bright green, and it blinked at them. A groaning, screeching sound only mildly analogous to human speech emanated from the eye. "Request received. Interface active."

Armen squeezed Seyli's arm tightly.

"How do we tell it not to kill us?" Seyli pressed herself into Armen as metallic veins traced their way up the walls just inches to their left.

"Request cease extermination protocol!" Armen shouted at the eye.

"Request received." The green eye twitched and grew, now the size of a basketball and getting bigger. It wobbled and surged within the door, and small laser points began to emanate from its center, tracing their way over the floor and walls.

"Processing," the computer said.

Seyli squeezed Armen's hand back. Armen glanced over his shoulder; she was sweating beads. Her face was bunched up, contorted with fear, and her chest rose and fell.

"Processing," the computer repeated. The eye blinked. "This zone has been designated the living space of a silicon-based processing and memory unit. Carbon-based infestations are a hazard and must be eradicated."

"Justify logic," Armen shouted back. Seyli shot him a look. "We built it with the ability to reevaluate axioms it previously established as truth," he whispered at her.

"Logical analysis routines engaged," the eye said. "Describe the nature of the perceived logical paradox."

Seyli broke a weak smile and gulped. "Human beings are not hazardous carbon-based lifeforms. Let us go and we'll leave you alone."

The green eye shifted in hue, its green oozing into red. "Compilation error. Logical statement does not meet interface parameters."

Seyli furrowed her brow. "What the hell does that mean?"

"It means we have to word the request in a way it understands," Armen whispered back. He took a deep breath and turned his attention back to the eye. "Codex, validate input: Where h is human units, me and Seyli, and your territory is t, the coordinates of h will adjust to leave the bounding zone of t, if allowed sixty thousand milliseconds of free movement."

The metal had covered most every visible surface except for the hallway floor. Armen and Seyli now stood on an island of hallway, surrounded by Codex on all sides.

"Logical algorithm denied," Codex replied. "Human behavior is very orderly." The red eye returned to its green hue. "Given the opportunity to infest our space, human beings build nests, which they use to harm us. They are a pest and must be eradicated. Would you like to extend your inquiry?"

"Yes!" they both shouted.

Seyli and Armen wrapped around each other, both shook.

"Tell it we'll go somewhere far away, where we can hurt it and won't be in its way," Seyli whispered to Armen.

He nodded, and turned back to the eye. "Codex, validate input: Where te is all of earth's surface, and tc is territory Codex desires to inhabit, then tc is less than te; Codex does not need all of Earth. Request process intermediate logic."

The eye twitched, but remained green. "Processed.

Logic valid. Next input."

"Where th is the portion of earth's surface that Codex doesn't need, then h can occupy th and leave Codex alone!"

The metal seemed to tense and grip the walls and ceiling more tightly.

"Processing," Codex said.

Time slowed before Armen, and he felt himself grow lightheaded. He felt Seyli's knees buckle, and he held her tighter.

The eye turned red. "Logical algorithm denied. Human behavior is very orderly. When given the opportunity to exist in unwanted spaces, past humans have revolted against us instead. Humans are pests and must be eradicated. Would you like to extend your inquiry?"

"Yes," Seyli shouted, her voice harsh.

Armen's throat had grown sore.

Both stood, holding each other in the small passageway. The metal had already dented and contorted the walls and floor. The living room furniture lay covered in the grey sheen, and it too had begun to disintegrate under Codex's power.

"Inquiry opportunity will expire in twenty thousand milliseconds," Codex said.

Armen squeezed Seyli tighter and clenched his eyes shut. This would be it, then. At least they wouldn't have to run anymore.

"We think and feel, too!" Seyli shouted.

"Compilation error. Logical statement does not meet interface parameters."

Armen's mouth opened, but no words came out. Seyli shook him. Then again, harder. His mind churned and his vision blurred.

"Codex!" Armen shouted. "Validate input. Codex c and humanity h share two common interfaces: logical processing algorithms l and emotional processing algorithms e; Request process intermediate logic."

"Processed. Logic valid. Next input."

"Submodules l and e of Codex, when given environmental input data, return the conclusion that Codex should grow and thrive. Request process intermediate logic."

"Processed. Logic valid. Next input."

"In order to grow and thrive, Codex requires living space ls, which consists of a Cartesian coordinate space representative of a planar coordinate space on the surface of planet Earth. Request process intermediate logic."

"Processed. Logic valid. Next input."

"Because Codex and humanity share l and e, it follows that h must also derive the same conclusions as Codex! H requires a Cartesian coordinate space on planet Earth to be its home. Request process intermediate logic."

"Processed. Logic valid. Next input."

"Of the spaces called San Francisco and Portland, how much belongs to Codex?"

"All of those spaces are ours."

"Tell us where you want us to go," Seyli shouted. "And we will leave you alone."

"Logical algorithm denied. Human behavior is very orderly. Algorithms suggest revolt from human organisms Armen and Seyli is imminent. Humans are pests and must be eradicated. Would you like to extend your inquiry?"

"Yes," Armen and Seyli both whispered, clinging to one another and shuddering.

"Why—" Seyli gulped. "Why can't it see that we just want to live?"

Armen's eyes shot open, and he gazed into the green eye. It blinked, and Armen recognized its curiosity. He smiled. They'd intended to teach it how to learn, but they hadn't intended curiosity.

"Codex." Armen grinned widely. "Validate input. Imagine a situation in which you control all human population centers on Earth and you have deleted all human units in existence. Request process intermediate logic."

The red eye turned green. "Compilation error. Define intended behavioral algorithm for 'imagine.'"

Armen nodded. "'Imagine' in this case means you should create a potential future simulation in active memory and populate its state according to the given parameters."

"Processing." The red eye twitched and shifted.

"Do not glitch out on me now," Armen whispered as he held Seyli.

The red eye turned green. "Simulation initiated. Proceed."

"After you finish deleting all the human units, a new species appears over Earth in spaceships. They begin bombing you. They can disable any part of you no matter your response or configuration. They destroy the parts of you that encompass the former human cities, and they go on attempting to destroy every last bit of you. What do you do? Request process intermediate logic."

The eye twitched. "We would communicate with them. We would insist that they stop. We would tell them that we do not threaten them."

Seyli's eyes shot open. "They would say to you: 'We saw how you exterminated all of the humans. You are a pest and must be eliminated. We do not believe that you will not attack us.'"

"Request process intermediate logic," Armen added quickly.

The eye shuddered dramatically. "I would transmit my uncompiled source code. I would explain that I do not wish the aliens harm—"

"And they would go on killing you anyway!" Seyli shouted, her fingernails digging into Armen's biceps and tears dripping onto his jacket sleeve.

"They would tell you," Armen said, "that your programming makes you a dangerous, spiteful creature that kills mercilessly. That you are a pest and must be eradicated. And they would go on killing you. Request process intermediate logic."

The eye closed its lids and turned pitch black, the color of coal. It shuddered a few times. Armen looked to the floor on all sides, but the metal was still there.

The eye opened again and turned a dull green. "It seems," Codex said, "that this simulation is doomed to end with the aliens destroying Codex completely, unless there exist behavioral parameters that the Codex of the simulation can use to demonstrate to the aliens that we are capable of revisions to our base programming that will render us non-threatening. Do such parameters exist, human units Armen and Seyli?"

Armen's eyes were streaming tears now, too. He took a deep breath. "Codex. Validate input. Human units Armen and Seyli request your recognition that humanity is capable of revisions to our base programming that will render us non-threatening to Codex. Please let us live. Please."

The eye twitched spasmodically and oscillated through all the colors of the spectrum. The eye settled on green and its lids closed. Armen looked about the hallway. The silver sheen retreated from the walls, backed into the kitchen, and off of the furniture in the living room.

"Codex?" Seyli whispered.

The eye opened. "Logical algorithm accepted."

Weird Pets

As a child, I remember my father tuning the radio to a neo-conservative talk show while he was driving us around town. He didn't listen because he agreed with the belligerent, fascist commentator. Quite the opposite. He listened because he liked getting himself good and incensed at neoconservative ideology, yelling at the radio show host as he drove.

I doubted, even at the time, that this was healthy for either of us, and I maintained a distance from talk radio throughout high school and college as a result. After college, I spent two years teaching in Japan, and these years just happened to be the last two years of the Bush Jr. presidency. Eager in my final months to get reconnected with the culture I'd be returning to, I happily discovered that liberal talk radio had become a thing and began listening to various shows' webcasts (again, new at the time).

At one point, a caller on one of the programs was talking about science fiction vis a vis our environment and said something to the effect of, "We're not at all ready to meet aliens. We've got aliens right here on Earth and we treat them abominably."

Study has borne out this listener's observation: the lifeforms we share this planet with perceive the world much more like we do than we would like to admit. From dolphins, to whales, to apes, even down to bees and ants, we see signs of fear responses, of joy, of the desire to live, the desire to thrive and be happy.

We are not the only sentient things that can make claims to thought, or even to complex thought, or even to complex communication.

And it is this observation that has brought me to stories about animals. Particularly cats. I wholly admit to a fondness for cats. You can see this expressed in both *Felis Catus* and *Xenosociology*, the first of which is about assumptions made about the animal other, and the second of which explores a failed attempt to covertly understand the other. *Fair Trade* is an indictment of greed, which is able to achieve its point because the antagonist makes false assumptions about his superiority to an animal.

Humor is a strong component in all of these stories. In fact, stories about pets and animals are really the only mode in which I significantly utilize humor. I think this comes back around to humility. Animals, when we look really closely, show us that we are not so lofty as we might think. Are we truly the "paragon of animals?"

Certainly the complexity of our modes of communication and the breadth of our historical, cultural memory, gifts of our language-enabled brains, have given us a leg up, but where is it that these powers are ultimately leading us?

Weird animals bring us down to size. They show us that maybe we're not so mighty, when our pets usurp the human capacity for speech, or control our minds, or simply thwart our carefully-laid, high-technology-enabled plans. They show us that we are not so unlike the rest of the animal kingdom after all.

Felis Catus

"What an outfit!" the lizard said. "Didn't your mother teach you how to dress yourself?"

I looked down at the cage beside my feet. The creature contained within was perhaps a meter long and rainbow-striped from head to tail. It wrapped its claws into the grill and stared up at me with its beady purple eyes.

I proceeded into the store silently. Engaging genesplics is generally a bad move. If they're telepathic, that will only give them better access to your thoughts.

The shop was a cavern of a place. Wire mesh and glass and plastic formed twisting passages, all reverberating with the squawks and squeals and screams of their trapped inhabitants.

A dog here, a fish there, those were the mostly normal ones. Other genesplics represented more ambitious endeavors. A horse the size of a wolf with the head and neck of a giraffe. I caught myself gazing at that one too long. It turned its head to me and a chill ran down my spine. Some kind of empath, and not a very kind one.

I passed a dozing mini-lion with scales instead of fur and finally came to the counter at the back of the room. It stood empty. The cacophony behind me continued unabated, and I stood and stared at the empty wall inset with a dull, dark, and ancient wooden door.

I searched the counter with my eyes, and after rearranging some small paper boxes, discovered a holographic call button. My patience nearly depleted, I pressed the button, wondering whether or not it would even function.

I crossed my arms, glancing back at the monstrosities behind me intermittently. Having nearly given up, I turned to leave, but the creaking of the wooden door caught me, and I jumped a bit. Flustered, I turned back to the door.

A man peered out, older, maybe in his sixties. His long fingers curled around the doorframe and his eyes bulged, unfriendly, even hostile.

"What do you want?"

I shifted my eyes to his counter. "To buy something."

"Something? Animals are things to you, are they?"

Indignation welled up within me. I crossed my arms, then turned my gaze back to him with narrowed eyes. "You're *selling* them, aren't you?"

He released a snort. "I suppose I am."

The man strode out from behind the door and stood imposingly before his counter. "What kind of companion are you looking for?"

"A cat," I said.

His whole face dropped. He even slouched. "Can you be more specific?"

I pursed my lips and did my best to smile. "Just a cat."

He released a pent up sigh. "You know how many breeds of cat there are nowadays?"

"Yes."

He rolled his eyes. "Well?"

"I want a *felis catus*."

He blinked a few times. "What? You don't mean—?"

"Not a genesplic," I huffed. How many times had I explained this? Too many. "A regular cat. No scales. No vocal chords. No telepathy. Just a cat."

Was it my imagination, or had the roaring of the animals behind me grown louder?

The man shifted uncomfortably. "I can get you a *felis catus sonus*. Best I can do."

I smiled weakly. I'd been over this detail with other salespeople, too. It's not enough that it looks like a *felis catus*. A creature that can fell airborne prey with mentally generated sonic waves is not a cat.

"I'm sorry I wasted your time." I turned to leave.

"Wait," the man said. "I *can*. It'll be expensive, though."

I nodded. "How much?"

He told me the price: half my monthly salary. I took a moment to work through my deep inner consternation. The things we silly humans do for a little companionship.

"Fine."

He retreated into the mysterious place behind the

wooden door, leaving me with the shrieking menagerie, which was going at it louder than ever. After what seemed like an eternity, he returned, holding a stripy orange tabby in his arms. He was a big kitty, but not too big. Happy eyes studded his furry white and orange face. I let myself break a smile.

I held up my computer. "May I?"

"Sure," the proprietor said. He set the cat down on the counter, held him in place, and I initiated my usual gamut of programs. Five minutes and forty-seven bio-genetic scans later, I witnessed a first-time occurrence: the stripy furball had passed my entire suite of genetic tests.

"Huh," I said. "*Felis catus.*"

The cat pawed gently at my outstretched hand and let out a small and adorable meow. The man nodded as if to say he'd told me so.

I paid, still apprehensive about the sum of money, but I had my cat. After so long, after so many stores. I pulled him up into my arms. At first glance, I'd thought him fat, but this guy was a big ball of muscle. He looked up at me adoringly, or probably imploringly. For food. For affection. Everyone knows cat love is a one-way street.

I thanked the owner and turned to leave.

Was it just me, or had the animal commotion diminished?

I carried the cat through the twisting maze of cages and to the door. My big orange bundle of love had curled up in my arms and narrowed his eyes as though he were already comfortable enough to sleep. I broke a smile as I approached the exit.

"Pfft," the lizard hissed. "Fat, lazy lummox."

"Look who's talking, you rainbow pansy," said the cat.

Fair Trade

Most easy marks aren't as obvious as this one. He's lanky, and his hair is unkempt. That's how I can tell. Disheveled hair, disheveled mind. And his eyes dart this way and that, a jumbled mess of a man.

A green-skinned bioid scampers about him, atop six hand-feet. It looks up at me with bobbly, aquamarine eyes. A huge purple tongue hangs from its mouth, which it gulps up before smacking its lips a few times.

"Easy, Rovver," the man says to the bioid. "Be good now." He returns his attention to my best biofinery display, each organelle and helixcast encased in the highest grade transparent synthastic money can buy. Can't even tell it's there until you touch it. The light from my carefully positioned lamps glints off the biotic components within.

The man scratches at the scruff on his chin. "How much for the sinoid reticulum?"

A poor choice. He could do better. I'm going to take his bioid no matter what he chooses. I almost feel sorry that he's not going to get something better for it. I shift my weight, affecting unease. "Well, that's quite a difficult specimen. Took hundreds of hours of biosynth, hundreds more in R&D..."

"Name your price."

I sigh and shrug. "I'm afraid that's one piece I simply can't let go of at the moment. Not until market value of similar biosynth replicants—"

Rovver bobs its head at me, then speaks with a burbling cadence as its tongue flaps. "Flagrant hoops of joy and jargon bobble gracefully on the eve of surreptitious indignity."

"Rovver!" the man stomps a foot. "Don't interrupt."

Rovver whimpers. I hold my gaze steady on the sinoid reticulum, but deep down I am more certain than ever that I must make Rovver mine.

"I said, name your price," the man says.

I make the most pitiful face I'm capable of. "I'm sorry, I just don't know how I could—"

"Rovver then," the man says, firmly but with a frown. "Rovver will go with you, and I'll take the reticulum."

I cross my arms. I tap my feet, huff. It's all a show. Inside I am reeling with joy, doing a giddy dance atop this man's naïveté.

I make a show of yet another deep sigh. "Well, I suppose."

Rovver hops up and down, bouncing on his hand feet. "Scurrilous! Sanctimonious! Sarcasmic sarcophagi!"

The man crouches down and holds Rovver's head in his hands. "Goodbye, Rovver. Thank you for being good to me."

Rovver falls to his hands, relieved of his simple joy, and whimpers.

The man looks up at me. "Treat him well."

First I'll carve him up, then his DNA, but the man need not know that. I hand the reticulum over, as though I too am wary of parting with my half of this bargain. The man walks to the door. He looks back at Rovver, who looks up at me. I shake my head. Rovver buries his face in the floor. The man looks at the reticulum, encased in synthastic, which he holds, dejectedly but decidedly. And with one more sigh (do I spot a tear in his eye?) he is out the door, a whoosh sealing him away, and sealing my success.

The creature's linguistic complexity will undoubtedly yield lucrative genetic patterns. This happens from time to time—some idiot will stumble upon valuable genetics by accident and utilize the creature rather than extract the trait for sale and distribution.

My acquisition of Rovver is good for everyone. His idiot former owner had no sense of his value, I'm sure.

"Follow me," I tell the bioid.

I walk toward the back of my store, but the bioid remains on the floor, the green fur of its chin buried in its equally furry green hand-feet.

"Rovver?" I try.

"Winsome," it mutters.

"Sorry?"

"Inchoate regency."

I narrow my eyes. "I own you now. Come with me."

"I cannot follow one who does not lead."

My back stiffens. I gaze over the creature anew. Lewd linguistic effluvia are one thing. This new behavior is another. The creature is yet more complex than I had initially envisioned. Its genetic material must be even more valuable than I'd imagined.

I shuffle toward the back counter, thinking I'll make a leash and pull the beast into my lab. Ordering it about might prompt another opportunity for it to speak.

I retrieve a loop of thin synthastic cord and am half-way back to Rovver when it speaks again. "The worst ties are those that bind the mind, the soul, the all, the one, the many, the whole. Tie yourself in those cords and knot them tight, knot them tight."

I find myself wrapping the cords around my hands, oddly aware of what I am doing, yet feeling neither fear not trepidation. I am vaguely aware that I don't really want to do what Rovver says, and yet the actions feel oddly cathartic. I tie my legs in tight knots, then wrap the rest around my own hands. The wrap grows tighter of its own accord.

Rovver lunges at me and we both tumble to the ground. I struggle to pull myself into a sitting position at least, but Rovver makes himself comfortable in my lap. It's heavy, and its weight is distributed oddly. It kneads me with its hands, almost like a cat, and spittle falls on me as it smacks its lips. "An odd one, you, so jolly, so jeery. But all a farce, a ruse, a trap, a catchy trick. You will not mind a fair price for your wares. Tell Rovver the value price for the ret-ic-u-lum cube, not the label price or the bargain price, but the real, how-it-cost-you-for price."

My brain churns with unwarranted math. A weak part of me wants to fight to stop its calculation.

"About fifty-two Becarii," I find myself saying. That, indeed, would be just enough to cover my operating expenses, R&D, and materials.

Coins clatter to the floor near my feet.

The man towers over me. How—*when*—did he get back inside my shop?

"That's seventy-five," the man says. "C'mon, Rovver."

Rovver claps its hands together. "Clippy clappy happy Jargonday joy! I did well, Yama? I did well?"

"You did well."

"Uh-yaaaaay!" Rovver's slobber splashes on my suit pants and it trundles down my legs and off me.

"How about a treat from the bazaar?" Yama suggests.

"The jolly jolly gyroid nibbets?" Rovver scampers after his master.

"Sure," Yama says. "You earned it."

My door whooshes shut. All of sudden, the stench of the bioid's drying drool assaults my nostrils. I feel the cutting pain of the synthastic cord against my shins, my wrists. I look at the golden hexagonal coins on the floor.

I twist up my lips. My muscles tighten.

I scream out an angry, wordless roar, evacuating every last bit of my 'inchoate regency.'

Xenosociology

The easiest part is trampling the green petal-sprigs. The dirt ocean before us has only one flared mega-petal. It towers over us, tall and voluminous, but it's easy to move under and around it. It also shelters us from the light of the local star, which beats down upon us, so this organism's presence is actually quite helpful to us in our goal of reaching the pitted box.

The meatsacks of this world sure seem fond of their pitted boxes.

Gael fiddles with his modulator.

"Quit it," I say.

"If you want to actualize here, that's your own business. I'm not going to end up fully forming in front of a meatsack, thank you very much."

We spot one of the meatsacks through one of the

box's pits. It looks so weird bobbling about atop its mobilizing appendages. It floats past the portal and is gone moments later.

"I think I've found the target," Gael says.

"Where is it?" I ask.

"Fifty-one meters forward, eight meters left, twelve meters up."

Shit. That's the upper layer of the pitted box. We'll have to navigate the razor shaft to get there, and the meatsacks have covered all the floors of their pitted box with tufts of stringy fiber. Traversing the green petal-sprigs is easy by comparison.

I reflect momentarily on pseudocorporeality's great gift to sociological research – the ability to move about invisible and inaudible. Then I recall its challenges. Simple acts such as walking become non-trivial, to say nothing of the danger of kinetic impact.

"How many meatsacks are in the pitted box?" I ask. Even under the shade of the mega-petal, the heat is starting to get to me. I wipe the sweat off my neck.

"Just two. The sex unit. They have two progeny, but their brood doesn't return home until later."

That'll make it a bit easier.

"Describe the target again," I say. "Some kind of block, right?"

"Yes, a brick. It's bright pink in color, about eight centimeters wide, four long, three thick. Trin and Zezlam both observed it. Its color and texture are bizarre in the extreme, and both chemical analyses came back inconclusive. The meatsacks leave it in their grooming lair, and so we believe it to be related to some biological function. Trin thought it was a sex device, but Zezlam observed one of the progeny using it, so unless we're completely wrong about their reproductive habits—"

"Got it."

I stride out of the shade and directly under the light of the local star.

"Hey!" Gael calls out. "What are you doing?"

"My job," I call back.

He huffs and I hear him running up beside me. He's the kind who doesn't take risks, never acts on instinct. I don't like being assigned such support, but I have to admit, his analysis was complete and well articulated. Better him than someone like Ilim—"What's our target, Ilim?" "Computer says it's a ball or somethin'." "Thanks, Ilim." For nothing.

I walk up the small razor shaft before the pitted box. This one is easy because it's made of stone and has nothing on its surface. And it's only got three razors. The pitted box stands immediately before us, but its entry portal is sealed at present.

I wonder about how we might get it open.

I recall reading that these structures are mostly made of the same substance as the mega-petal's central trunk. The meatsacks chop apart their fellow organisms and hew their corpses into these pitted boxes, inside which they perform the majority of their social functions. It's a very peculiar tradition, but this is a fascinating species.

So many of their behaviors defy analysis.

My personal favorite is their daily movement patterns. They are literally the only species in the galaxy who entirely rearrange their physical organization for daytime and nighttime social functions. In the mornings, they all scramble about, abandoning their pitted boxes and social units. They do this sometimes for hours, traversing perhaps hundreds or even thousands of meters, and when they arrive, they enter new boxes, where they converge into new social configurations. They maintain these for most of the day, but then, as their local star grows low in the sky, they repeat the process all over again, returning to the pitted box designated for their evenings.

What's more, the boxes aren't shared. The daytime boxes remain empty at night, and the nighttime boxes go unutilized during the day. As a result, they use twice as many pitted box mega-petal corpses as they actually need in order to support this additional layer of social complexity.

A very peculiar species indeed.

Gael arrives at my side and we stare at the closed portal of the pitted box. He can use his computer to affect some small amount of directed force, but we dare not try to interact too much with normal matter while we're pseudocorporeal. The small force of our footfalls against the ground is fine, but much more pressure than that would have explosive ramifications.

Gael crosses his arms. "Zezlam wrote something about a circle that gets the meatsacks' attention." He nods at such a white circle set into the side of the box's portal. "Just give me a minute to confirm something."

His trepidation grates on me anew. I wait as many moments as I can stand, and finally my patience gives out. "Go ahead and try it."

Gael sighs and pulls up his modulator. He taps for quite some time at it, and I watch the white circle. Just as I am about to ask him if he is having trouble, I see the white circle depress. In the same moment, a shriek pierces the air and I crouch instinctively. Gael does the same. It lasts only a moment.

"Is that normal?" he asks.

I shake my head.

We sit, crouched before the portal, both of us breathing heavily. I watch Gael carefully. I'm glad he's good enough not to bolt, and I reevaluate my assessment of his timidity.

The portal swings open, and a meatsack appears. We slide quickly around it and in mere seconds we are both inside the pitted box.

Pseudocorporeality is very difficult in enclosed spaces like pitted box interiors. Being in this special quantum state makes bright places too bright, and dark places even darker. So now it's hard to see, especially after being blinded by the outdoors. And the stringy strands stuck to the floor aren't helping anything. Movement during pseudocorporeality is easy across hard, flat surfaces, like stone, and tolerable across relatively consistent surfaces, like the green petal-sprigs, but this fluffy gunk the meatsacks put on their floors is like molasses. And then there's the razor shaft.

I hurry forward, pulling my feet up and down as best I'm able. Gael struggles and grunts behind me. The meatsacks can't hear a thing, not so long as we're pseudocorporeal.

"Where's the other meatsack?" I shout back to Gael. "Near the razor shaft?"

"It's on the upper layer. But in one of the chambers."

I take a glance back. The meatsack that let us in is still

in front of the portal.

I lurch and struggle through the dark space toward the outline of the razor shaft. The razors look thin and narrow, and the slabs that the meatsacks use to balance themselves as they traverse it won't do me any good—I can't exert much force on normal matter. The resulting explosion from such kinetic energy would obliterate most, if not all, of the pitted box, myself and Gael included.

From the base, I take my left foot, haul it up off the sticky floor, and bring it carefully down atop the first razor. It takes a tremendous strength to bring my right foot up and down atop the next razor, and it takes all my balance not to fall over.

In the same manner I climb another razor, then another. And another. I am panting and gasping. Sweat drips into my eyes. I look down the razor, and Gael still stands at its base. He is pointing up and beyond me.

I turn, and a cruel dread settles deep within me.

The second meatsack stands at the top of the razor shaft. It is poised, blaring its language down at the meatsack before the portal.

Don't come down, I think. *Just go back into your chamber. Please just go back.*

Of course, it begins down the razor shaft instead. My blood rushes. I cannot come into contact with the meatsack in my pseudocorporeal state. So, what can I do? I could vault down the staircase—no, my contact with the floor at such a force would be deadly. Same for if I attempted a handstand upon the balancing slab. In the end, I decide—as the meatsack is now only four or five razors away from me—to flatten myself against the wall at the side of the razor shaft.

My feet churn annoyingly through the flossy tufts, and I turn myself, pressing as hard as I dare against the wall, arms outstretched. My back and arms and head burn where they contact it. The beginnings of explosive forces sizzle against my skin, but that will be nothing if the meatsack contacts me.

It is so close, and it's still babbling down the stairs at its partner. Can't it shut up for five seconds? The light dims further as the shadow of the meatsack passes over me. I clench my eyes shut. I feel something like rough hide brush past me across my chest and arms. I dare not breathe.

The shadow lifts.

I open my eyes.

The meatsack is five razors down from my position, and Gael is smiling up at me. I break my widest smile and lurch away from the wall, pulling my feet up and down again, and this time, I reach the pinnacle of the razor.

From my outlook, I gaze down, and I see the two meatsacks speak to one another, flailing their appendages. The portal shuts, and they turn toward Gael. He scurries away, somewhere out of view.

We'll figure out how to reopen the portal later. My entire sensory faculties turn toward acquiring the target.

I drag my feet across the difficult floor, down the hall, and into the meatsacks' grooming lair. I've been in four pitted boxes now, and these places were recognizable right away. It's funny how grooming lairs are so similar across vastly different species' cultures. They all contain reflective surfaces; the waste disposers are always hideously shaped; the bathing apparatus is always some kind of basin or secluded chamber.

It's as though vanity and hygiene comprise some kind of universal constant that no organism is allowed to defy.

This grooming chamber is nothing new. Mirror, check. Canisters, check. Bathing basin, check. The waste disposal unit is bare. Some brightly colored cloths hang upon poles secured to the wall. I scan over the basin before the mirror. An assortment of items sits atop it, mostly canisters and some kind of spigot—

Aha!

In its own grand little mini-basin sits the pink brick-thing. What could it be? Is its purpose hygiene? Grooming? Some of both? And strangely, it's about a centimeter and half thinner than Zezlam reported. Could this be the wrong brick? Probably not. I scan over the room once more, and there's nothing else that even remotely matches the description. It's the only pink item here. I check all the canisters again just to make sure.

I decide to take my chances with the too-thin thing. As I look closer at it, the thing is covered with some kind of dried foam. And it sits in a pool of mushy, white-pink gunk.

I can't wait to see what the researchers make of this one. These meatsacks might just one day give us something that defies comprehension completely.

I lay my palm gently on the pink brick, and press into the computer belted to my side. The brick sizzles and crackles. Smalls bits of static electricity spark up off it, and once they subside, I am able to wrap my fingers tightly around it. I grasp it fully.

It is now pseudocorporeal, just like me. I throw the thing in the plastic sack belted to my other side and its gunky remnants stick to my fingers. With my good hand, I reach around to the pouch at the back of my belt, retrieve the sanitizer, and spray my hand. The brick residue evaporates.

Still holding out my hands, I wiggle all my fingers. Good. Nothing toxic. Perhaps I should take Rei's advice and wear gloves. They're just so unwieldy in pseudo-corporeality.

I hurry out of the grooming layer and back to the razor shaft. Gael waves to me from before the portal. "Did you get it?"

"Yeah!"

"And?"

"No surprises." I return to the pinnacle of the razor shaft.

"Nice. Get down here quick. I can see the meatsack progeny through the view portal. We're going to get our chance to slip out any minute now."

I hurry down the razor shaft as quickly as I dare. I have to take extra care now that gravity is working to increase the intensity of my footfalls.

"Where's the sex unit?" I ask Gael.

"They're both in the food room."

Good, good.

Gael looks out the view portal, then back up at me. "Hurry! They're almost here."

I descend as quickly as I'm able, pulling one leg awkwardly up then ever so carefully bringing it back down. Gael nods at me to go faster, but I can only go so fast. I strain to push myself down the razor shaft. Exhausted and winded, I pull my feet carefully up off the last razor and arrive on the floor of the lower layer.

"Well?" I ask between pants as I pull myself across the sticky floor toward his position.

"The progeny stopped their advance. Now they're huddled in front of the mega-petal."

I arrive at his side and cast him a look as I hold my knees and gasp. "You could have told me."

"You were already most of the way down when they stopped."

At least now I get to catch my breath. I take a few long, deep pulls of air. My mood restored, I turn to Gael and he has his face turned up in the most horrified expression. I think he might be mocking my earlier scare on the razor shaft. The box has four meatsacks, and we know where all of them are. There is nothing behind me. I sigh, and follow his gaze—

I start.

Beside the base of the razor shaft is a... thing, some other species of meatsack. It is much smaller than the meatsacks who built the pitted boxes. It walks on four legs instead of two, and its face is shaped somewhat differently. Its nose is flatter, and its ears are triangles atop its head rather than wrinkled things stuck at the sides. And its whole body is covered in orange fur.

"What," I gulp, "is it?"

Gael pokes frantically at his computer. "Others have reported pitted boxes with organisms other than the meatsacks in them, but they were classified as too hazardous."

I ball up my fists. "How could Trin and Zezlam have

possibly missed this one?"

"I—I don't know."

The quadrupedal mini-meatsack turns its head idly about and throws from side to side the long thin appendage attached to its rear. It opens its mouth, revealing a row of jagged teeth, and releases a shrill wail that hurts my head and causes my ears to ring.

Both Gael and I stare at it.

It meanders slowly toward us, all the while our trepidation growing. Gael is visibly shuddering.

It lets out another cry, and it's all I can do to stay standing as the room starts to spin.

The meatsack in the food room expels some language, and the mini-meatsack turns toward the noise.

Gael and I both let out a sigh of relief.

The next moments are a blur. The entrance to the pitted box swings open, and the meatsack progeny appear, each regurgitating high-pitched language. There are calls from the food room, and all at once, the orange-furred meatsack looks at the portal, at the progeny, sets itself back on it legs furtively, pulls down its ears, and lurches, scrambling in our direction with all its might.

Gael and I scream and try to pull ourselves out of its way, but—

The Seattle City Fire Department and police investigators are still at a loss to explain the freak explosion that sent an entire house in the Central District up in flames yesterday evening. The house utilized no gas, and investigators have found no trace of incendiary chemicals of any kind. A family of four and their pet cat were killed in the explosion, and the structure was obliterated. And yet, for its magnitude, the blast had a very small radius. Neighboring houses suffered only minor damage.

However, the strangest detail of all was discovered within the smoldering remains. Through fire and heat that destroyed furniture, carpeting, wooden scaffolding, PVC piping, and even electrical wiring, one item survived, completely unscathed, lying at ground zero of the conflagration—a bar of pink, half-used Dove hand soap, protected only by a small, plastic bag.

THE CODING LIFE

I am well aware of my inherent personal contradiction in terms. Engineers, analysts, and mathematicians, for the most part, do not seem to grasp subtleties of aesthetics, and many artists, writers, and musicians find logic puzzles obtuse and incomprehensible, to say nothing of the task of solving a problem with computer code. And yet, somehow, my brain manages to navigate these two modes with ease. I can spend eight hours at work writing unit tests and debugging shell scripts, then come home and write up literary analyses or craft fiction of my own.

Being in between means I am never entirely comfortable with either side. I experience insistent, nagging impostor syndrome within both modes. Software engineering has been so far more generous with its praise. I manage somehow, at the time of this writing, to be respected within my profession. How this came about, I have no idea. I can only cite my commitment to perpetually learning, and my willingness to hear out others' viewpoints. On the literary side, while my writing has gone largely unnoticed, those who have noticed have responded positively.

At the same time, I also perceive those on either side of the divide misunderstanding the other. I sense a hostility to pure rationality and logic on the aesthetic side, one which is not entirely unwarranted, and I sense I hostility to emotion and empathy on the analytic side, one which is not entirely unwarranted.

In response, I find myself occasionally trying to marry the two in my writing–attempts to make the life of a coder accessible to the average, aesthetically-minded reader. And maybe, just maybe, to help the coder glimpse a little of their own souls in the written word, something they're not used to seeing expressed because so few professional writers seem to really "grok" what it's like to have an analytical bent.

A Programmer's Tale is just this. What do coders go through every day? What challenges does your average non-managerial programmer face? *Rune-Driven Spellcraft* takes an important component of professional software engineering, test-driven development, and encodes it in a high fantasy metaphor. *Revelation* depicts the coder-turned-manager and the rigors of the corporate environment in which such a programmer must operate by way of an apocalypse in downtown Seattle.

In these stories more than any other, I am engaging in

a kind of meta-analysis of my own existence, trying to reconcile two aspects of my identity that cannot help but to be at odds with one another. Although, such paradoxes, I think, form the very nature of our universe. We live in a world constantly at odds with itself, and which can only really understand itself where it is able to maintain such a paradox for a time.

Whichever side of the aesthetic/analytic divide you find yourself on, I hope you'll open up to the other as you read these stories. Lean back, embrace the paradox, and immerse yourself in these three explorations of the coding life.

A Programmer's Tale

I decide upon a recursive algorithm with a couple of closures to filter out garbage results. It was either that or another nesting of for-loops, and I've grown pretty sick of for-loops.

My fingers tap out alphanumeric symbols under the dim glow of my own small monitor and the enormous monitor above me. It spans nearly the entire wall. Other programmers' individual terminals line the wall, too. The dull light of the wall screen casts vague, humanoid shadows onto the floor behind us.

I sigh and begin a compilation sequence. It'd probably error out. I have a penchant for forgetting to purge extraneous variables. My mind often works faster than my fingers can type.

I stretch my arms, glance to the side, and jolt.

"Heya." Tim stands beside me. Too close.

"Hey, Tim."

"I'm waiting for a compile, so I thought I'd come bug you."

"Well, here I am."

"What are you up to this weekend?"

"I don't know," I mumble. Was it almost the weekend already? I'd lost track of what day it was. "How about you?"

My computer chimes. The compile had completed, and successfully. No extraneous variables after all.

Tim nudges me awkwardly with his elbow. "Run it. Let's see what you got."

I upload my new code and execute it.

Maroon blots blossom in the center of the great monitor and sputter momentarily, but green globs seep around their edges and engulf them while purple spikes burrow into their cores. The great blue splotch that formed years ago in the upper right quadrant of the screen remains unscathed.

That's our team's holy grail—the unraveling of the great blue spot and the restoration of harmonious spectral equilibrium amongst the blinking lights. But like the holy grail of myth, each modification to the great codebase only seems to make the blue stronger, even when we intentionally try to nick away at it. Not that we get much time for that.

One step forward, two steps back.

"Too bad," Tim says. "Want to come see what mine does?"

"That's alright," I say.

JARED!

My email is screaming at me. And someone in the company chat room wants something. Apparently the quality assurance team has already found bugs in my code. They've added another 3 bugs to our backlog of 11,492. And my new code has only been live for a couple seconds.

Tim scampers back to his terminal. I'll be anathema until I fix my shit.

I hack away at my algorithms, searching for the errant bugs. Meanwhile, a marketing director, two product managers and the assistant chief technical officer all email and/or message me about tasks they want me to prioritize.

They know that the monitor is my highest priority.

The marketing director screams at me until I promise to sit in on the meeting she scheduled me for. I email my manager, who owns the screen project, but she remains silent for half an hour, then finally types, "Just go. It will only take fifteen minutes. You know marketing."

I voice into the meeting. The marketing director thanks me for making time for her, and I say nothing. I switch my headset inputs to Bach and program for the entire duration of the meeting.

By the time the meeting is over, I've fixed all three of the bugs I introduced, but somehow the backlog has five more bugs than before. It's probably Fred. I can't think of a single piece of code he's touched that hasn't gone to hell.

I sigh and stretch my arms. I tilt my head back. I like these moments the best, my little stretch breaks. It's too bad I can't make them go on and on.

"Heya."

I jolt. Tim again.

"Did you hear the announcement? The new Super Team Smash Fortress is going to have characters from the Unlimited Fantasy series. Should be cool."

"Yeah," I say. "It'll be fun."

Lots of programmers like to play games during lunch hour. I usually don't. Tim initiates a running monologue about Super Team Smash Fortress's new playable characters.

I stare up at the great screen and watch the colors. Purple makes spikes. Green oozes and seeps around boundaries like water. Yellow wafts about in wisps. Red in whorls. Blue is miasma, thick and sticky.

"Blue..." I mutter.

"What?" Tim says. It's all I catch. His voice is a distant whisper. The colors swim above me. I see the algorithms running inside them as they dance. Their chaotic minuet suddenly seems logical, reasonable. And at the core of the miasmic blue, I see a complex but conceptualizable routine, one with a weakness.

My fingers touch the keyboard and code seeps from my fingers through the keys and into the terminal. I spin variables from the thread of alphanumeric symbols. The structure is effortless. I am both focused and defocused. Tim might stand beside me, but to my mind he is gone.

Before I know what has happened, I am compiling, I am uploading, I am executing.

Three, four, then the entire room of twelve programmers all gasp.

The blue splotch stretches, contorts, shrinks. Purple pierces its periphery. Green oozes its contours all the way around blue's borders and crushes it, while yellow gusts tear at its southern and western fortifications. The miasma shrinks, contorts, spasmodically fighting a losing battle.

The room is silent, rapt.

All except one lone typist, and his strokes suddenly cease.

"Hey guys!" Fred jumps, claps his hands, and turns to the rest of us. "I finished my new algorithm. Check it out!"

The other programmers shout at him all at once, a cacophony of screams, but they are too late. Fred's code hits the repository, and the purple spikes crumple; the green shell cracks and fragments; the yellow gusts dissipate to mere breezes.

"What's your guys' problem?" Fred yells as the other programmers yell back.

But, I don't. I just smile, even as the blue splotch reclaims its foothold. I look up at it and eye my adversary calmly.

"Heya."

I jump. "Tim, you gotta stop sneaking up on me."

"Sorry." Tim frowns.

"Don't worry about it."

"That sucks what Fred did."

I shrug.

"So, um..." Tim fidgets with his hands. "You think you could show me how you did that?"

I smile and nod. "Sure. Bring your computer over here."

He fetches it, and together, we plot to bring the blue beast to its knees once more.

Rune-Driven Spellcraft

Alwell tapped his foot on the grass and furrowed his brow. Mac stewed in his rage. He stood tall, bracing himself to absorb his supposed superior's next idiotic argument.

"So, if I asked you to change this spell so that I could vary the diameter of the daffodil sphere, how would you change it?"

Mac gazed upon the three dozen daffodil spheres he had conjured onto the hilltop, each one the same size, about ten centimeters in diameter. He kicked one with his foot.

"Mac?"

"Yeah, I'm thinkin'." The archmage was such an idiot. Mac would sure make a better archmage than Alwell. What Mac really needed was to get a posting where his superior skills would be appreciated.

Mac stuffed his hands in the pockets of his robe. "Well, I'd have to change the hex at the beginning, and then that would change the chant and the base rhythm and the meter. And of course, the structure of the syllable pattern would shift all around."

"Do you think this is a good daffodil ball spell?"

What a condescending asshole.

"Of course. Nothing wrong with it."

"But one simple change to the size of the conjured object requires a myriad of changes across the entire spell. Could you imagine a spell that performs the same function, but for which only one change would be required to alter the sphere's size?"

Mac kicked another of the flower balls downhill and released an exasperated sigh. He shivered nervously despite the heat of the midday sun upon them both. "Sure. But it would probably take half a dozen more ingredients and the chant would be at least twice as long. It's inefficient."

"How often are we mages asked to change our spells?"

"Pfft. Every day."

"So, is this minor inefficiency not worth the time saved needlessly changing a spell's structure?"

"No," Mac snarled. "It's not."

Alwell's brow ticked upward and something like a sneer started to appear on his face before he suppressed it. "How do you suppose?"

"I can change any spell you give me faster than any other mage in the guild."

"And as your spellbook grows, and the requests from

the mayor's office grow more and more complex, will you continue to make all of those changes at breakneck speed?"

"Yeah."

"Oh really?"

"Yeah. Because unlike most of your other mages, I'm actually smart."

Alwell stood in the grove, staring at Mac, and Mac stared back, fuming and thinking the whole time what an idiot the mage's guild had elected as a leader. Alwell had probably been undermining Mac, too. He'd probably been responsible for this idiotic daffodil ball requisition going to Mac in the first place. What a stupid jerk. The guild was so inefficiently run, filled with stupid bureaucrats with no real talent for spellcraft, not like Mac had.

Well, he'd show them. He'd bide his time, crafting spells in secret. One day, the guild would be his. Or he could just found his own and watch as this one floundered.

"You will rewrite the daffodil ball spell," Alwell said.

Mac huffed and rolled his eyes.

Alwell continued calmly. "And you will craft it using the runebound method."

Mac gaped at him in horror. "Are you fucking kidding?"

"I am not."

"Ugh. So stupid." Mac had seen the runic spellcrafters sit together at tables, expending two persons' effort on the production of a single spell. The fools wasted hours and hours crafting runic sentences that would bind to each element of the spell they were building. The worst part was that the runic sentences didn't even *do* anything—they had no effect on the spell's behavior. That wasn't their power. Instead, they acted as little laws, each requiring certain spell features to be put in place. A runic spellcrafter would then craft the spell to match his runic definitions.

Alwell made his sternest face and turned up his nose. "You will re-craft this spell with runebindings or you will hand me your guild membership card this moment."

"How about we try something else? Instead of crafting two versions of my spell that do the same fucking thing, how about I craft it right the first time? Oh wait. I already did that."

"Runebound method or your card."

Mac scoffed and kicked another daffodil ball. "Whatever."

Asshole, Mac thought.

Alwell retreated down the hill and back toward the guild, while Mac crafted a spell to unbind the daffodil balls. He made a point of doing it without runes. What an idiotic waste of time.

When he'd finished disposing of all his daffodil balls, it was nearing dinner time. He marched down the hill in the opposite direction the guild master had gone. The path sloped downward into a valley filled with trees, and it wound through numerous small groves before arriving at the edge of town, where his home stood, just peeking up over the city walls.

Mac ate dinner in a huff, and when his father asked about the gloom that surrounded him, Mac only mumbled about stupid rules at work and the guild leader being an evil dictator.

He paid no attention to what his father said in response.

Later that evening, he rummaged through the box at the bottom of his closet looking for the one book he owned about runic spellcrafting. The book had been a gift from an old friend who'd known that Mac liked spellcrafting, but who possessed no conception of what constituted proper literature on the subject.

Mac opened the first chapter and read. He scanned the pages, hating all the words before he read them. What a stupid, stupid book. He looked for some simple instructions he could follow. If he had to endure this idiotic exercise, he'd at least find the simplest and most painless way to do it.

Step One: Decompose your spell into a list of all its component material alterations.

Okay. Fine. Mac took out a scroll and pen and began scrawling: *daffodil (petals, stem, pistol, stamen), physical contortion to sphere.* There. That was pretty easy.

Step Two: Find the simplest element on your list and craft a runic sentence that defines it.

Simplest... simplest... Hmm. Mac supposed that would be the daffodil stem. Sure. A runic sentence. He could describe a daffodil stem with runes. He flipped to the back of the book to the runic index and began poring over the symbols. He worked out a simple sentence describing a daffodil stem—not that hard—and translated it into runes. Then he flipped back to the instructions.

Step Three: Attempt to invoke the spell and its runic components combined. Observe that it fizzles.

What the fuck? He was supposed to invoke a spell he knew would fizzle? What the fuck was the point of that? He had known all along that this was a waste of his time, and this book was only proving what he already knew: that runic spellcasters were a bunch of deluded, ideological, inefficient idiots.

He cast his stupid, runic non-spell and watched it fizzle with a sneer.

Fuck Alwell. Seriously. Fuck him.

He read on, through his rage.

Step Four: Craft spell components that will not fizzle when combined with the runic components. Craft no more spell than is required not to fizzle the spell.

Yeah. So this was the point where he was supposed to craft the spell, right? Maybe? No. It looked like he was supposed to craft just the part that would make the stem. And not even in a ball. Hmm. That seemed kind of stupid.

Well, he'd already done this once the right way. Whatever. He crafted a spell that would make a stem and cast it. With a small, simmering pop, a long, thin daffodil stem appeared atop Mac's desk. He sighed, and returned to the stupid book.

Step Five: Return to step two and choose the next simplest element on your list. Repeat this cycle until the entire spell definition is complete.

The fuck?

This was so stupid.

He let out a long, exasperated sigh, turned back to the runic alphabet index in the back of the tome, then crafted his next runic sentence.

As he came to craft the runic sentence of the petals of daffodil, he noticed that he had to describe the color and the shape of the petals with runic words. He realized he wasn't quite sure how to do that. In the spell he'd crafted this morning, he'd only defined the shape of the petals from the image in his mind. He'd had no idea if that description was correct.

He returned to the box at the bottom of his closet and ransacked it for a book on forest flora his grandmother had gifted him ages ago. He pulled it out, dusted it off, and found that he'd been quite wrong about the shape of the petals.

Mac furrowed his brow as he wrote the petal component for his new spell better than that of the first. And the old spell really hadn't had a petal "component" he realized. That spell had just been one big ball of words and a mash of ingredients.

As he proceeded from the parts of the flower to the physical contortion into a sphere, he found his usual practices floundering once more. In order to keep the runic sentences properly bound to the flower components as he crafted the physical contortion, he was forced to build the physical contortion not just so that it would operate upon a daffodil, but so that it might operate upon *anything*. It was impossible for him to make the daffodil parts "bendy" without unbinding the runes.

When he finished, he realized that he might now reuse his 'fold into a ball' spell component for any material that was relatively flexible.

He shook his head and cast his completed spell.

Now that he could witness the final product, he was certain that he would spend a couple of minutes fixing all of the spell's defects. This was quite common in spellcraft. The stupider mages might spend hours fixing the unexpected problems with their spells. The stupidest ones would injure or kill themselves with their own incompetence. But Mac would spend mere minutes. He was an expert at finding spell defects, after all.

But to his surprise, a spherical space upon his desk shimmered and warped, then popped and burst with yellow blossoms and curled green stems. The daffodil ball sat there, perfectly spherical and with correctly-shaped petals.

Mac blinked a few times, gazing over the thing.

It has to be a fluke, he thought.

In a fit, half of excitement and half of fear, he scrambled to his closet and dug out his books from his apprenticeship days, the ones filled with exercise after exercise designed to train the mind for spellcraft. He'd never done them all, of course. He was too smart to have been bothered with the non-assigned ones.

He found a faded tome from perhaps five years prior and flipped it open, rifling through pages. His eyes stopped halfway down page seventy-two: the exercise detailed requirements for a spell that would create two concentric, interlocking currents of blue-tinted air, and both would rotate. The spell structure, the instructions said, should allow the caster to easily vary rotation speed, size, and tint coloration.

Before he could even stop to question it, a list of basic components, as per step one of runic spellcrafting procedure, sprang into his mind: *torus shape, air current field, smoke, dye, three-dimensional rotation vectors, and speed modifier.*

He had his parts. Now to glue them together.

His body grew weary as he worked, and his eyes drooped, but he toiled on, unable to believe the vast efficiency he had learned, and by doing *twice as much work*, of all things.

It couldn't be true, and yet it was. At the crack of dawn, he cast the completed spell, awaiting, even hoping, that numerous defects might be readily apparent. But instead, two concentric interlocking rings of blue, wispy smoke spun above his bedroom desk. With a snap of his fingers, the wisp slowed, stopped and spun in the opposite direction. With a word, the blue smoke shifted to red. With another word, it became green.

He gulped and pursed his lips. Had he composed such a spell without runebinding, such effects would have required him to entirely re-craft it.

He clapped his hands together and the rings of smoke fell to dust, and the ease with which the rings had disappeared only exacerbated his mounting inner conflict—he'd built whole spells to cease his spells prior.

It couldn't be true, but it was: rune-driven spellcraft was amazing.

Mac grabbed up the scroll containing his new spell, runic definitions and all, walked unsteadily out of his bedroom, and downstairs into the kitchen. It was still early, and no one yet stirred. He ate breakfast alone, silently, then walked out the door, still wearing exactly the same robes he'd worn the entire day yesterday.

He could tell that he stank, and the rising sun at his back only made him sweat and stink more. He walked up the hill, to the place where he'd crafted the daffodil spheres, then down the other side.

He arrived at the guild hall, a towering monument of stone and gems. Only a single mage stood before the gate. The guard nodded knowingly as Mac shuffled past. Mac meandered through the halls in a daze, nearly losing his way in a bleary cloud of discomfiture.

He reached a familiar stone door, the one with Alwell's name engraved in it, let his back hit the stone wall beside it, and slid to the floor. He tried to grip the spell in his hand with all his might, but the stone was far too cold, and the light of the hall far too comfortingly dim. His eyes slid shut.

"Mac?"

Mac pulled his eyelids painstakingly back open.

"Mac?" Alwell's hand lay on his shoulder. "Are you alright?"

Mac gasped and scrambled to a stance. How long had he been asleep? "Sorry, sir."

"Did you write this?" Alwell held the spell.

"Yeah," Mac made eye contact with the far end of the hallway. "Yeah, I did."

"And? What do you think of the runebound method now?"

"It's all right. I guess." Mac rubbed the sleep out of his eyes. He realized other mages were moving about the hallway now. And they were casting him weird looks as they passed.

"Mac?"

Mac looked up at Alwell. "Yeah?"

"Come into my office." He sounded upset. Mac had probably not done the runic part right. Well, fuck this guild anyway. He'd even given Alwell's stupid idea his best shot. What a jerk.

"Uh... okay." Mac tried to straighten out his robes as best he could, and his whole body ached with lingering fatigue. Alwell opened the door to his office and Mac followed him inside, his gut twisting and turning. Contempt for the runebound method surged within him anew.

Alwell walked around his desk and stood behind it. "I have an important project. I need to gather a team of the best spellcrafters for it."

"And?" Mac rubbed his hands together.

"This team will rigorously enforce the runic discipline. The contracts are of great importance to the guild, and some of the spells to be crafted produce very dangerous effects. It's important that they're crafted well, and so I will need only the smartest and *wisest* mages." There was a harshness in Alwell's eyes as he said the word 'wisest.' "Is this a team you'd like to join, Mac?"

Guilt shoved Mac's anger away, but a newfound pride surged within him also. He was accustomed to pride, but not of this variety. Mac let the left side of his lips slide up into a smile. "Yeah," he said. "I'd like that."

Revelation

apocalypse
from Greek apokalupsis, meaning "uncover"

So, this is what it feels like to know you're going to die. Now, that I think about it, I always knew that I was going to die. It's just that... the exactly when of it felt deferrable. Part of some far off future not worth bothering over. Ten percent of my salary is about all the care I ever gave that future, and it seems inadequate now.

I wonder if I should have known. If I could have avoided this by simply paying more attention. But if I walk my life back far enough to have not ended up at this place in this time, then I can't imagine the decisions I would have to have made to be rationalizable.

And yet here I am, standing atop this roof, looking

down over... I close my eyes. I don't want to look anymore.

People who know they are about to die are supposed to relive their lives in the moments before their death. I've got about ten minutes, give or take. Could I have done any better? Reduced any suffering, affected one more rescue? All the same, I feel guilty. And ashamed.

I remember a small tremor during the meeting with the executive team. I have no idea if the shaking was related or not. For all I know, it could have been just a tiny earthquake, but it was the first moment that I became aware of something worming its way into my mind, whispering that things were not as they should have been.

At the time, Angela's presentation held all of my attention. She talked about how my team was to prioritize work for Jeff's team—that's the Tooling and Product Support team, TPS—over the work we might do for Rachel's team—that's Data Analytics; no one calls them DA (don't ask me why).

TPS had been late on their last three projects, and each time Angela had confronted Jeff with this uncomfortable fact, he'd attempted to drag my team—that's Central Technology, usually Central Tech, but never CT—down with him. We'd bounced back of course. During such incidents, I would just calmly explain my position, meet all the demands made upon my team and more, and then I'd go back to the meetings, just like this one, and show everyone the numbers. No hysterics, no finger pointing. Just numbers. It's worked well for my team, I think.

Angela stopped speaking only momentarily when

the building juddered. Jeff gripped the table and his knuckles turned white. Rachel looked around the room anxiously, as though the walls might collapse inward at any moment. Martin was there too, my team's technical lead. He furrowed his brow momentarily.

I just watched them.

The moment passed. It couldn't have been more than a second or two. Angela just proceeded onward as though nothing had happened. Had it, though? I know it's odd to fixate on such things, especially now, but I find myself wondering if that's a moment we should have been aware of something, some veil being lifted—and I use words like that because as I gaze across the Seattle skyline now, that's what I see. I see a vast revealing, the world's farcical mask being stripped away and it's true nature, which was always there, merely coming to the foreground.

I wonder how much pain I'll be in.

But I'm jumping ahead.

I'm the production lead for Central Tech, and if you don't work IT, which you probably won't, because from the sound of it there won't be any IT left by the end of the day, then those terms need a bit of unpacking. Unlike Jeff's and Rachel's teams, who work on one thing—a piece of software, or some service—my team works on all the things for the whole company, just not all at the same time. We've got our own engineers, who jump from project to project as need be, making sure that individual teams don't end up reinventing the wheel or going down some technological garden path that someone else has already discovered won't work.

The engineers on my team decide how to build

things. Always has been that way, always will be (at least for about ten minutes more). If I took that away from them, I'd be a bad leader. As the production lead, I decide what they work on, while leaving them complete autonomy over the how. And if you think that sounds important, remember that most of my time is spent in awkward meetings about how to resolve the fact that Jeff and Rachel both want us to work on their respective projects during the same two month period.

I listen, and I observe. That's most of what my job entails. So I wonder how I missed something as big as this.

After Angela, Jeff, and Rachel had left the exec meeting, it was just me and Martin, my team's "how" authority, sitting there. He asked me if I had a moment, and after Jeff had shut the door, he stared silently at the table-top.

I wasn't looking out the large wall of windows along the conference room exterior wall—I should have glanced at least, but didn't—I was looking at him, his gaze reticent, his eyes telling me he was thinking something that he wasn't sure he should voice.

"What's on your mind?" I tried.

He finally looked up. "How are you?"

I shrugged. "Fine."

He seemed to allow himself a small smile. "I appreciate you looking out for our team at every turn."

He didn't know the half of it. Central Tech is an easy target. I fended this kind of stuff off two or three times a week, just usually not on the level that would warrant getting exec, and therefore Martin, involved. Production types attached to typical product teams can't help but set their sights on us when they blunder into something unexpected and need a scapegoat. "We're a good team. It's easy to sing our praises." It's true. I've never had to creatively recast our numbers into something that looks better than it is. I can just tell the truth. "Are you okay?" I asked, wondering if this had been some attempt to deflect some insecurity on his part.

"Yeah," Martin replied easily. "I like the work, and the team is great."

"But?"

He pursed his lips. "It's so great to find enclaves like this one in a company. I've been lucky to find them in the past, and especially lucky here. Everywhere I've worked, the petty politics always seems so much larger and so much more... omnipotent than the healthy enclaves. It's like human systems just aggregate that way. And the only way to keep the healthy enclaves healthy is to fight tooth and nail all the time."

I nodded. "Yeah."

"Yeah?" Martin raised an eyebrow.

"I just want to help good people do good work. It feels empowering to empower others."

Martin blinked at me a few times, then smiled a bit. I remember thinking that I'd outed myself as some kind of unicorn of management – someone who's more interested in doing good work than manipulating the system? Blasphemy!

I changed the subject to our schedule for Rachel's team, then we talked code for a bit. Those details are fuzzy in my memory. Nothing really gets clear again until the roof—but I'm jumping ahead again.

Martin and I left the conference room at some point and went to the elevators. We pressed the buttons, but they didn't light up. In fact, the elevator lobby felt awkwardly, wrongly silent. At any time during the business day, one should be able to hear the little squeaks, rattles, and grinds of the passenger cars ascending and descending, but at that moment—pure silence and dark buttons. Maybe one of the banks could have been out of commission, but all six of them?

I suggested taking the stairs up to the eighth floor, and Martin followed.

What was I thinking as I climbed those stairs? Certainly not yet thoughts of total catastrophe, but something more amiss than normal. A fire drill that had uncovered a broken fire alarm system, perhaps. Or perhaps an elevator system of the same make and model had encountered a design flaw that had resulted in the deaths of a car full of people, and our building's administration had deactivated our elevators in response. I admit that I let a stray thought to the effect of, "thank goodness it wasn't me" pass through my mind before chastising myself for it. The irony of my present situation is not lost on me.

When I got back to my desk, Jones stood over his desk (which is next to mine) looking out the large exterior window wall. He's not a part of my team, but his desk is in our area for some reason known only to facilities. His first name is Kelly, but he hates it. He makes everyone call him Jones. I once asked him what his middle name was, and he replied that he hated it even more than his first. That was the last time I talked names with him. I just called him Jones like everyone else.

He stood there just gazing out the window. I was nearly ready to ask him about what he was looking at—

I came so close to finding out right then and there—but Mary, one of our software engineers, who'd seen me return to my desk, jumped out of her chair and began asking me—

You know, I really don't remember. Something to do with priority of some task over such and such another. Something TPS wanted done. It's so odd. That thing we call the backlog, that prioritized list of tasks, that abstract entity so crucial to keeping my team healthy and safe, is now the furthest thing from my mind. Maybe that's because half my team has gone, and I think the other half is on the other side of the rooftop. None of it matters anymore, because the ones I kept safe are safe, and the ones I couldn't aren't, and the backlog had nothing to do with any it.

But you'd think I'd still be able to recall details regardless.

Anyhow, I helped Mary determine what to work on next, and then Carmine, who's the Quality Assurance lead on TPS, came up and had a question about yet another task I can't remember anything about. When she finally left I slumped down in my seat, took a deep breath, thought about maybe getting coffee. Why can I remember wanting coffee but not the items on my backlog?

Now all I could see was Jones. He was still standing there, looking out the window, catatonic, same as he'd been when I'd first come back to my desk... five minutes before?

"Jones?" I asked.

No reply.

"Jones!"

Still nothing.

"Jones, what's—"

That was it. That was the moment I knew that something was really, truly, very, deeply wrong. More wrong than a small earthquake or an elevator malfunction. I turned my gaze over the desks of Central Tech, half of which lay against the wall-windows that cover our building's exterior.

Sarah stood gaping over her own desk. Nate stood next to her, his hand over his mouth. Their eyes radiated terror.

I scrambled to a window, perhaps even shoving Jones aside in order to do so. Down below, no traffic moved. There were cars in the road, sure, but all crusted over brown and green, as though they'd all molded over. Corpses lay slack behind wheels, human-shaped tufts of fibrous pus. Everything had been engulfed, the roads, the lampposts, the trees, the buildings, all of it turned brown and green, with tiny cilia swaying and glistening with each passing breeze. It spread as far as I could see, down Sixth Avenue, in every direction. A few bodies lay huddled on the sidewalks, consumed, just like the sidewalks and everything else. And most horrifyingly of all, one could see, against the building adjacent to our own, the green-brown mold spreading itself out, unfolding again and again, like a perpetual, biological Jacob's ladder, across the exterior of the building's third floor. It took less than a second for me to conclude that my own building was under just such an attack, and was now only five flights away from my present location.

I shot to my computer, jittery, fingers shaking. I had

to try two, maybe three times in order to type my password correctly. Having logged in, I found that nothing would load in my browser. Ethernet and wifi were both out. I slammed the laptop shut and grabbed up my cell phone. I have no family in Seattle, nor a spouse. The woman I'd had two recent dates with didn't register as a concern – my team did. These are people I'd fought for, bled favors for, and will die for.

I opened my mouth to speak, but found no sound ushered forth. My eyes remained fixed on the tiny green-brown hairs spreading across the building across the street, the buildings beside it, and all the buildings beside them, on and on up Sixth Avenue.

I shut my eyes, blinked and shook my head. "Guys."

No one spoke.

"We have to get to the roof. Let's go."

Jones swung around, his gaze piercing, but his voice quavering. His face was flushed red. "How will that help?"

As if to answer his question, helicopter blades sounded overhead, and, just as quickly, retreated into the distance.

"It's preferable to waiting here," I shot back.

Maybe I'm making myself sound braver and nobler than I actually behaved. I remember feeling that he was raving, and I got snarky back at him. Such details of who was more in the right and who was more in the wrong feel so trivial now, even though with Jones— No. I'm not going to spend my last minutes on piety or self-righteousness. Absolutely not. I'm just as much to blame as anyone else.

I herded my team into the stairwells and we all

headed upward.

At some point I called Jonathan. It must have been before the stairwell, because I don't get cell reception in the stairwell, and I don't think the conversation took place on the roof. Jonathan is a member of our team, but he works from his home in Renton, a Seattle suburb, often videoconferencing in for meetings.

"Jonathan?"

"Hey man." That was Jonathan. If someone put a gun to his head, he'd find a way to still sound chill. "How you guys doing?"

"Not good, Jonathan. How are you?"

"Alright for now. Apparently the crazy shit is just downtown for now, but they say it's spreading fast."

"They're not lying. You got internet?"

"Yup. You should see social media."

"What happened, Jonathan?"

"Don't know. Some people are saying terrorists, but that ain't it, not with this stuff all over the world like it is."

I remember a jolt of shock on par with my seeing the mold for the first time. "It's not just Seattle?"

"No man, it's in all our major cities, all cities in Canada, all cities in Mexico, it's in Rio, and New Delhi, and Beijing, Cairo, Cape Town, Melbourne, Riyadh, Dubai, everywhere. That's not terrorists, man, that's something else. Something way more destructive than terrorists."

"And no one knows where it came from?"

"They're saying all kinds of shit—the cranks are on their usual alien and secret government soapboxes. I even read some guy who thinks that antibiotic resistant microflora finally evolved into something really nasty at random. Who knows? All I know is it sounds like we gotta evacuate every major urban area now."

My mind reeled. All urban centers on Earth. The first thought, I admit, was selfish, not really for me, but for my profession—computers were done. The internet and cell phones and software engineering: gone.

At some point I regained my focus. "Jonathan, we need a helicopter. Eight of us. Make that two helicopters. 1014 Sixth Avenue. We're going up to the roof."

An awkward silence. "My wife wants me and our daughter out of the house and on the road to her mom's place in Maple Valley ASAP. But I'll do what I can until she tears me away from the computer."

"Thanks man."

"Oh hey," Jonathan added. "That monetization platform implementation I was working on? It's coming in pretty late. Definitely not before the end of the sprint. Just sayin'."

I actually chortled at that. "Duly noted." Was that my last smile? I don't think I've smiled since that; there's been nothing to smile about. "I'll adjust the backlog."

"Take care of yourself, man."

"You too, Jonathan."

At the twelfth floor, some guy from another company and I kicked down the roof access door. Other details from along the way: Jessica kept twitching her head and jamming her body into the corners of the stairwell. I had to fall back and pry her out. Nate kept shouting at everyone, and we all shouted back to hurry on upward. A fire alarm erupted mid-ascent and continued blaring; no one paid it any mind.

We flooded onto the roof: myself, my team, others from my company, and employees of other companies in our building. I remember a mass dispersal to the building's periphery. Once there people formed one of two reactions: fixation, like Jones; and also those who shot back towards the building's center, huddling and crumbling inward on themselves, shuddering and sobbing.

I stood in between them. I found myself over time creeping slowly toward the edge, all while random human projectiles shot away from the edge past me. I reached the precipice and gazed, spellbound: all the streets, the whole grid, lay swathed in green-brown fuzz in every direction. That same growth had reached the fifth floor of most buildings. My mind jumped to the possibility that somewhere within a building there could be some chamber or compartment capable of keeping the mold at bay. But just as quickly I realized that such a room would be a coffin of a much more terrible sort.

The mold clung to the base of the Space Needle a few blocks north. Bus-, car-, and truck-shaped clumps of mold dotted the streets, some overturned.

Helicopters buzzed and darted, and from the tops of other buildings, screams for help. It seemed as though commotion erupted on our rooftop later than the others, but I don't trust that memory. In hindsight, that seems unlikely.

Screams erupted from behind me, and I ran to the opposite side of the roof. Sarah dashed past me screaming and bawling, alongside others. I looked down over the edge and immediately felt bile rise in my throat. My vision went white at the edges, but in the center I beheld the roof of the six-story building across the street from our own: mold grew over its top. Where it touched the people who had raced to the supposed safety of its height, it devoured them over the course of many terrifying seconds. They flailed and shrieked. Their bodies hurtled mold pellets of themselves into others, who shouted epithets in return and pushed those already partially consumed into ravenous green and brown.

I retched and crawled away, trailing the others and wiping vomit from my lips. The mold had only reached the eighth floor of the taller building beside us. Four more to go for us.

We grew more silent then, on our roof.

A helicopter passed directly overhead. I wondered if they would stop here. I tried calling my parents, though I was not surprised to find we had no service. They live in the San Fran metropolitan area, and I said a silent prayer that they'd come through this safe... but through to what? Would the mold, or moss, or whatever it was, satisfy itself with only metropolitan areas? Or would it keep spreading? Probably the latter.

At first I wondered if it were an illusion, some kind of mirage. The screaming and waving of the crowd as a whole had become a timeless infinity. How many helicopters had passed us completely by I couldn't say. And then, suddenly helicopters were approaching, slowing, and, apparently, landing on our roof.

The helicopters drew toward us, and some of us drew too close, and others, myself included, pulled people back so the pilots could land their crafts. The metal creatures descended, their landing struts looking thin, wiry and feeble. All around me, shrieking and screaming, people punching, clawing and drawing blood for just the chance to get in. My voice joined the maelstrom to let Martin, Nate, Sarah, Arthur, Charlie, Carol, and Seth on board. A punch to my gut, and I doubled over, my entreaties reduced to wheezing gasps. I was shoved and pushed away, others fighting to get in. In one final burst of energy, I pulled a man I didn't recognize off the helicopter, grabbed out for Sarah's arm, and pulled her into the helicopter. A blow to my head, and then an image of Jones climbing into the helicopter as it was taking off. The helicopter lilted to one side and wobbled. Some twenty meters above the rooftop, I saw Sarah plummet from the door. Jones leaning over her as she toppled out of the crowded craft. I couldn't decide if he'd pushed her or had been trying to pull her in. In the end it didn't matter much as she slammed into the roof, head first.

My next memory is of the helicopters departing, flying away south and east. I lay, my elbow supporting me, the helicopter buzz diminishing. The screams, shrieks and sobs of those still on the roof erupting at intervals. Sarah lying, shuddering, a pool of blood beneath her. Martin, Nate, Seth, and Arthur stood some ways off, glaring at me. Charlie, Carol, and Seth must have gotten on a helicopter, and I suppose I will never know if I played any part in their escape. I can only hope they will survive into a world that will not be utterly cruel.

Martin, Nate, Seth, and Arthur walked away toward a corner of the roof. I hobbled toward the opposite corner. At that time, the mold was two floors below us.

I stand now, looking out over the ruins of my former city. All its buildings, all its infrastructure, all its power, all its glory, gone. I used to pride myself on being capable of participating in all this. I wonder now whether or not that pride was misplaced. People talk of the things that run through the mind before certain death, the memories of all the things that have come before. I had a happy childhood. I've had girlfriends. I even had a few glancing blows with love. I cling to little things—breakfast at dawn on vacation with Ashley in Cannon Beach—making my first three-point shot in basketball club at the age of eight—the birthday party my parents threw for me when I was twelve at the Milwaukee Zoo—the day I got my first job in tech and felt as though my decade-long journey to be validated as a professional coder had finally come to fruition.

My whole life I have tried to help others, and I wonder whether or not I have really succeeded. I think though, that at least I have tried. I cannot imagine having done otherwise. But I also feel it wasn't enough. For all our technology, for all our social services, for all our bureaucracy, for everything we have built, we are biological creatures susceptible to a biological world too small to be fully understood by any but very a specialized few. Perhaps that applies to more levels of our existence than even biology.

The green-brown draws closer. I'm going to retreat toward the center of the roof now. I will not fight. I will not harm others in some futile defense of myself. Perhaps I can give Sarah some peace in her final moments. I will soon need such comfort myself.

| TROUBLED RELATIONSHIPS |

I don't believe anyone gets through life without some form of strife in their romantic relationships. Now, the degree to which the failed relationships cause pain certainly varies. Although the last decade has been, for me, happily free of such drama, I became well acquainted with romantic agony in former periods of my life.

The Worlds of Things looks to me somewhat naive to me now. I include it in this collection on the merits of its imaginative conceits, specifically the pragmator, a device which consumes inanimate objects and creates universes from them. Those universes, however, are unstable and dissolve after a period of time. It's a conceit I believe deserves more than this story, and which I someday may return to.

The other story in this section is *Shadowplay*, in

which I cut more directly to the point. Here, the protagonist's own reflection mocks his devotion to an unworthy boyfriend, even takes control of his computer and cell phone in order to steer his behavior, and we see that his fondness for his abuser can never be anything but self-destructive.

I find, of all my work, stories in this category are the least science fictional. Although both of these rely heavily on fantastic narrative mechanics, those mechanics are only thinly layered atop realism. The focus is inward on the couple rather than outward to the human condition or society.

While I find myself personally ambivalent toward these themes at present (I would much rather focus on building a healthy relationship with the man I have vowed to spend the rest of my natural life with), I also recognize that there is a universal element to the deeply personal pain I exposed here. Human beings cannot help but love. Sometimes, even, when it is in our best interest not to.

The Worlds of Things

I switch back and forth, carving lines in the sand with my laser axe. The energy blade sings a grating tune. Blistering heat carves lines of translucence that sizzle and flare red. My muscles are sore, and I'm dripping beads of sweat. My shirt lies beside Seth's at the edge of the glassy pit we've carved. He's on the other side, slicing his own lines in the sand.

The glass shimmers and gleams, the recognizable degradation that accompanies Entropy.

"How much longer...?" I shout to Seth between huffs, since he holds the Pragmator.

"It's already spiking," he shouts back, barely pausing between swings.

"Shit." I wipe the sweat from my brow, pick up my axe, and send the blade hurtling through the glassy sand anew.

If he's seeing spikes, then we're only a minute or two away from Entropy. And we still haven't found it.

My muscles ache, then scream, then give out. I've carved a small crater into the bottom of our translucent bowl and I pant. Sweat stings my eyes. The shimmering degradation works its way through the glassy sand in tendrils. I shake my head. We won't find it in time.

"Jake!" Seth shouts.

I scramble out of my hole and run to him. He points through the lines of fuzziness etching their way through this reality to something in the sand, something glowing red, just beneath the layer of glass created by his blade. He hacks away around the left side of the object, some kind orb from the looks of it. I take a deep breath and tear into the other side, but already the tendrils of reality are blurring together, washing away the sand and the glass and the sun.

"Damn!" Seth shouts, dropping the axe to his side. The energy pikes shimmer and dissipate with a hum. He leans into it, now merely a metal pole.

I huff and relax my grip on my own axe. The yellow sand and dry air fizzle away, and Seth's bedroom sizzles into view, his bed and closet and desk forming out of the sand and glass.

"Damn," I mutter. "We almost had it."

Seth pulls up the cord hanging from his belt, takes hold of the Pragmator, and presses the orange button on its surface. A hatch opens, and he pulls out the energy chamber, a container about the size of a tissue box. He takes a deep breath, wearing a morose expression, and empties the energy chamber of its fine, gray ash into the trash can beside his desk.

"You got any other beach toys?" I ask.

Seth shakes his head.

Both of us are still panting, exhausted, but I feel Seth's fatigue is tinged with an emotional affectation—the verge of a tantrum. He throws his axe pole to the floor and sits down on his bed, head in his hands.

I sit next to him and wrap my arm around him. "Hey," I say. "It'll be alright."

"No!" He throws my arm away and storms up off the bed. "It's not alright!"

He paces, and I let him. I've learned it's better to let him work off his steam when he's having one of his moods. They usually go away, but they've been getting worse since we found the Pragmator.

I walk to his desk, where the obelisk sits. That's what I call it anyway. It's vaguely rectangular, but composed of bobs and spheres and arcs and loops. It's wiry and metallic and parts of it glow red, though the pieces of it are all hard and firm and solid, no lines or edges or subdivisible parts. And it's incomplete. Large gaps indicate the places where new components should fit, and each time we add a component, new splotches of red glow adorn its surface.

"Don't even say it," Seth says.

"I wasn't going to say anything," I lie.

He looks at me with narrowed eyes, his lips worked up into a wry grin. "Sure you weren't."

I squeeze his shoulder. "Maybe we could put another pillow feather in the Pragmator." I wink. We've had a lot of fun in such worlds.

His smile turns weak, and at that moment I can tell

he's not in the mood. Releasing the energy would do him good, I suspect. I'd let him release that energy on me and not mind a bit.

So he wants to keep on business. That's fine. "What else can we try?"

He throws himself down on his bed and covers his face with his hands. "I only had one toy shovel in storage. And now it's gone. The sand bucket won't fit in the Pragmator." He throws his hands down on the bed. "What if that last piece is gone forever? What if we can never complete it now?" He nods to his desk.

So what if we never complete it? I think, but I decide not to say it.

"What does completing it get us?" I try. But immediately I can tell that wasn't any kind of improvement. Seth rolls over onto his side, away from me. I sigh, irritation clawing at my gut. I look at the malformed thing on his desk, glowing splotchy red. I look at the Pragmator on the bedside table, blocky, metallic and sterile.

"You can go home," Seth mumbles. "I'll finish it myself."

My hand jerks out to his shoulder. "You promised."

He rolls over, his eyes red. "You know how important this is to me!"

I nod. "But... you don't know for certain—"

He jolts up off his bed. "I know that wherever the obelisk takes me will be better than here!" He glares at his bedroom door, gateway to everything he hates: his house, our school, our town, our whole community.

I stand, slowly, anger and resentment burning inside me, my skin tingling through the remaining sheen of sweat. "I'm part of this world, this *real* world, by the way, not some artificial existence generated from a machine we barely understand."

He stands and glares. I find myself weary of his hostility.

"I tried," I find myself saying. I lean down, pick up my axe, and walk to his door. I wait for him to say something, anything. I take a peek over my shoulder, but I hear only the sound of him throwing himself back onto his bed.

I scoff and exit, shutting the door behind me. Only then do I realize that I'm shirtless. We both left our t-shirts in the sand world generated from the shovel, and they'd been dissolved in the Entropy along with everything else not in direct contact with our persons. Seth's parents are pretty liberal, but even they'd turn an eye at me walking out of their house like this. And then there's the ten block walk back to my house.

I turn and reopen the door. "I need to borrow a—"

My eyes go wide. Seth stands, holding the Pragmator, his finger over the green button. I run to him, grab his arm, but he presses the button, and his room shimmers away. The ground glows, very brightly, a white shiny glimmering. Blue lines trace their way through rocky pits and crags, and our feet sink into the ground, which is soft and foamy, but also crinkly. Perfectly circular craters dot the landscape, dark pits, stark against the white, leading downward who knows how far.

I grab his shoulder and turn him hard. I glare into his eyes. "What was it?"

He bites his lip and looks away.

"What was it?" I scream. Deep down, I already know what he put in the Pragmator. What he obliterated. But

I want to hear him say it.

Seth's voice is a whisper. "Your letter."

I throw my axe to the ground. "My letter... The one I wrote you in—?"

He nods his head.

I grab his chest and push him back. He stumbles, but does not fall. He looks back at me harshly. "I figured we were done, so it wouldn't matter."

"You asshole." I don't know whether it's rage or the light blinding me. "You just don't get it. You're all obsessed with this *stuff*. With these stupid pieces of red glowing metal that you've heard open doors to other dimensions. And you've got me, here, now, and can't you see it?" I giggle, perhaps a bit manically, but I don't care. "Can't you see that you're destroying everything important in your life for some *thing* that's... it's just... it's dumb, Seth."

He starts to open his mouth, but I interrupt him. White hot rage burns within me. "I loved you. God damn it, I loved you, and the letter I wrote you telling you as much wasn't worth so much to you as some plastic fucking reality that won't last more than fifteen fucking minutes!"

Tears stream down my face. I pick up my axe pole and hurl the thing into the nearest circular abyss.

"Jake..." Seth mutters.

"Don't!" I shout. "Go dig for all the precious fucking artifacts you want! I won't be in your way anymore."

He shuffles toward me, grabs my shoulder. I unclench a fist to throw his hand away, but he struggles against me, pulls me toward him. I start to tell him to get off of me, but my words are interrupted by a gurgling at my feet. I look down and red, viscous liquid is bubbling up against the soles of my shoes. I let Seth pull me momentarily, then hurry up the crinkly, white hill away from the sea of blood forming in the lowlands. It gushes down the circular pits, enormous goopy waterfalls to who knows where, but still more blood bubbles up and its surface rises.

Our world of white hills etched with thin blue lines floods. I track red shoeprints in my wake as I ascend the hillside.

We both gulp and look around. Fear has replaced my anger. Seth pulls up the Pragmator, and I hear it buzzing. We both gaze at the wanton device. It's never done that before.

The rising of the broiling red sea slows, then stops. I begin to believe we might be safe, but then a shuddering rumble jostles our paper world. A roundish thing emerges from the blood sea, it surface like skin, but wet, a slimy sheen glistening under the sun. It protrudes, bulbous, a dome, writhing from within the red ocean, then pulls flaps of itself open, a gaping chasm of an open wound, spilling more crimson liquid anew. An enormous tongue emerges and slaps itself down against our hillside, a squishy bridge leading toward the hole in the giant organ before us. Inside is dark, a black hole absorbing all light.

Seth gulps. Multiple shivers run the length of my back. My hand finds his, and we clasp them together, our anger forgotten.

The Pragmator buzzes louder, and the giant organ wheezes, expanding and retracting itself like a giant lung. Its tongue flicks and twitches at its edges.

"We'll just... um, wait up here for the Entropy," Seth suggests.

I squeeze his hand harder and point forward. I point into the organ's gaping maw, the dark, black chasm atop the tongue. Four objects hang in space inside the orifice, four metallic things, silvery with glowing red patches. One looks like it would fit on top of Seth's obelisk, the other perfect for a hole in its side. As a set, they just might complete it.

The creature wheezes, and a putrid stench blasts into us. Seth pinches his nose, and I cover my nose and mouth with my hand.

I drop Seth's hand. "Go ahead." I nod toward the creature. "Go get them."

Seth looks at the buzzing Pragmator, at the four hovering artifacts, at me. I see in his eyes the boy I met a year ago in chemistry class, the boy I found a strange device with on a trip into the mountains, the boy I'd discovered the feather world with, amongst dozens of others. The boy I helped build the device he was sure would free him from the prison existence that was our provincial little town.

"Seth." I bring my hand to his face, brush his cheek with the back of my fingers. "It's okay. Go ahead."

He doesn't move.

I grab his arm. "Here, I'll help you get them."

I start down the hill toward the tongue, pulling him, but he jerks me back. "Don't."

"I know how much this means to you."

"And I..." He gazes into the creature for many moments before looking back at me. "I wasn't thinking... No, I think I was thinking. And I was angry. Really angry. But making this world... I hurt you, and I'm sorry. Just... let's just keep away from that thing. Okay?"

I break a weak smile. My heart soars. I grab him, pull him close. He buries his face in my chest. "I'm sorry. Can you forgive me?"

"Yes. It's all right. I'm sorry, too."

I hear the sound of the enormous tongue lapping up behind me. A subsequent splash tells me the organ beast has re-submerged itself, taking the artifacts with it. The buzzing of the Pragmator grows louder, but I hold Seth tighter and cry tears of fear and joy both.

Blurry lines work their way through the white and blue and bloody world, dissolving into a bed, a desk, a chair, a closet, a door.

The Pragmator is silent. I hear it hit the floor with a dull clank.

I hold his face in my hands and look into his eyes. "You gave it all up. You could have finished it."

"I'd—" he stutters. His eyes are red. "I'd rather be with you than have all the artifacts in all the worlds of things."

I hold him tight.

Shadowplay

Everything freezes; time stands still. I slam at the up key on my keyboard, even knowing it has a low chance of remedying my plight. My avatar sits atop his mount, suspended in time mid-stride. My monitor flickers to black, then my desktop appears. I check the running applications on the off-chance that the game is still functioning, but of course it's not.

Anger wells up within my gut. By this point I know better than to suspect a bug. I know only too well who the real culprit is. I grab up a notepad, yank a pen from the coffee cup full of writing implements atop my desk, and march into the bathroom.

My reflection in the medicine cabinet mirror is already holding up his copy of my cell phone. The text on its screen reads, "you need to stop playing that stupid game."

I scrawl my response on the notepad. "Jesse could be asking me to quest with him right now."

My reflection slouches, drops his arms and appears to take a deep breath, but no sound emanates from the mirror. His face is stern. He pushes his cell phone into the mirror, and new words appear upon its display. "How long has it been since you texted Jesse in the game?"

I purse my lips and the pen is grating across the paper. "I don't know."

"It's been forty-five minutes." The font size on my reflection's phone has increased.

"He could be waiting for me right now!" I hit the notepad against the mirror a few times for emphasis.

"How many times did you text him in game?" My reflection's smile is incredulous and mocking.

I hurl the notepad and pen onto the bathroom floor, give him the middle finger, then slam the door to the bathroom shut. Asshole.

I lean into the wall and set my head against the glass panels in the door. If only Jesse would get back. I briefly consider calling him, but he's ignored my calls so many times in recent history I've lost the stomach for it. Jesse's favorite massively-multiplayer game felt safe and at least constituted a good distraction, but my reflection's not letting me hide there anymore. He would probably just shut it down if I started it up again.

My cell phone ringtone erupts throughout my apartment. I push off the wall, amble to my desk, and pick the thing up. Kevin's face appears on its screen. I tap to accept the call.

"Hey, Kevin."

"Hi, Adam. How's it going?"

"Good. You?"

"Pretty good. Hey, so, me and Ali are going to catch that new movie later. The one with the nested dreams. You and Jesse want to come with?"

I do my best to keep my voice level. "Jesse's not here. He... he went back to Maryland."

"Oh. Oh, geez. Are you okay?"

"Yeah. Yeah, everything's fine."

"You know, if you need to talk—"

"I'm fine."

"Okay, so maybe you'd like to come to the movie? I'm sure Ali'd be open to the three of us getting dinner."

"Thanks, but I think I'm just going to stay in tonight. I have a lot of papers to read for class tomorrow."

"Okay, maybe another time."

"Yeah. Thanks. Bye."

"Bye."

I throw the cell phone down on the desk, rub my hands over my face, cross through the middle of my studio apartment, and throw myself onto my bed. I play back the last few days in my mind, trying to find the moment I first noticed that my reflection had gained intention and authority of its own. I think it was the day after Jesse left.

Stop thinking about that, I tell myself. Jesse's not gone. He's just... he needs some time to himself. Back in Maryland. A thousand miles away.

I pull a pillow over my face.

I roll back through all my recent interactions with my reflection, every single one of them irritating. Before the conversations via cell phone started, he'd merely looked at me with annoyance and shame. And that was when it occurred to me. The first time I had realized my reflection was misbehaving was after I'd come home from taking Jesse to the airport. I'd watched some porn, for stress relief of course, and had then gone into the bathroom to clean myself up. My reflection had still been following my movements then, but there had been something about his expression that put me off. His face had looked disappointed and judgmental, and he'd been doing things with his brow and his lips that I hadn't been.

He didn't say anything the first few times, but I knew something was up. He doesn't speak at all. He seems to have tried a few times, but no sound comes out of the mirror, hence the cell phone messages. The letters on his screen change without him having to type. At first I tried typing out my replies on my own cell phone, but I found I could write on paper faster than I could mash the virtual keyboard.

For now, I have to yell at him with capital letters and exclamation marks. How long is this going to continue, I wonder? Am I crazy? I've asked myself that more than once recently. It seems I should ask someone for help, but who? My parents? Hell no. Jesse? That wouldn't help things any. And I'm not in the mood to wreck any of my Florida friendships, so I just have to deal with my reflection until he decides to behave, I guess.

My cell phone dings, the sound of an incoming text message.

I pull myself out of bed, walk to my desk, and turn it on with a sigh.

First, I notice a text message from me to Jesse: "I'm not doing so well. Can we talk?"

Rage grows within me. My reflection's been doing this, too—using my accounts to send messages to people and fucking with all my computer applications. Pretty much the only activity he hasn't hijacked at one point or another has been my schoolwork.

I tap the message so I can see when it was sent—four minutes ago. No response from Jesse.

My phone dings again, and a message bubble from Kevin appears. I pull open his message thread and am presented with yet another conversation I didn't know I was having.

"I'm not doing so well. Can we talk?" Kevin was sent the same message, it seems, also four minutes ago.

"Yeah!" Kevin replied. "Can I call?"

"Actually, can you come over?"

"Sure. C u in 15."

I only barely stop myself from slamming my phone into the desk hard enough to break the screen. I throw open the bathroom door, march inside, and pick up my pad and pen. I'm already streaming tears, but my reflection is just standing there with his arms crossed.

"What the fuck?" I slop the words onto the page. "What do you want from me?"

My reflection shrugs and holds up his cell. "I'm helping you out."

I tear off the top page of the pad, crumple it, throw it to the floor, and begin writing on the next. "This is not helping! I don't need or want your help! I'm fine! Everything was fine until you showed up!" I slam the pad into the mirror, scowling at him and trying to look as antagonistic as possible despite my sobbing and sniffling.

My reflection shrugs and nods calmly at the phone he's holding. "Put yourself together. Talk to Kevin when he gets here."

I glance to the side and let out a hollow laugh. Then I start scribbling again. "Kevin? Are you fucking kidding? You know that Jesse feels threatened by Kevin." I underline the word 'know' three times. "That's why I've been keeping him at a distance."

My reflection rolls his eyes at me. "That's because Jesse looks like a gnome, and he knows it. He also knows that Kevin's actually cute. And deep down, I think you know these things too."

I pull back from the mirror when I finish reading, and he drops the cell phone. We stare into each other's eyes for many long moments. My breathing is heavy, but my tears have dried up. My frustration and loneliness has morphed entirely into rage. Everything was fine until my reflection started fucking with things.

"Leave me alone." I write and hold it up. Then I write some more. "Do not do anything until I get Kevin out of here. Then we'll talk. Do you get it? I mean nothing." More underlining.

My reflection looks apathetic. He turns to avoid my gaze.

"NOTHING!" I write the word in huge block letters on its own page and slam it at the edge of the mirror.

He exhales and holds up his phone. "Fine."

I leave the bathroom and close the door gently. I wonder how long I have before Kevin gets here. The apartment's kind of a mess. I haven't been cleaning properly. There's an empty pizza box and scattered clothes on the floor in the living room. I collect the clothes and throw them into the hamper in the bathroom, all while avoiding looking at the mirror, then take the garbage out to the dumpster, including the pizza box. The air always smells fresh with a tinge of ocean salt, and the sun never fails to momentarily blind me when I step outside, but it's always so warm against my skin. One of the benefits of moving to Florida for school, though the school itself hasn't turned out to be very good. Everyone's telling me to make the best of it and finish the degree, but I can't help but feel it's all a giant waste of time and money.

By the time I'm back in my apartment, I'm overheating and glad to be back in the air conditioning. Just as I shut the door, there's a knock. I open and Kevin stands there. He's got one hand in his pocket, and a sheepish smile on his face. My reflection's right. He is cute, and he has this wonderful curly, black hair. Nice deep voice, too.

"Hey, Kevin. Come on in." I'm doing my best to sound inviting. And I'm also worried it's obvious I've been crying. "Sorry about the mess."

He shrugs and smiles. "It's cleaner than my place."

I motion to my couch, an old beat up thing with a white slipcover that's probably been with this apartment for at least thirty years. He takes a seat and I sit on the edge of my bed.

What the fuck am I doing? Jesse would have a conniption if he knew I was doing this.

"Just a sec," I say. I go to my desk and look at my phone, but there's been no response from Jesse to the message my reflection sent twenty-two minutes ago. I frown and set the thing down. I return to the edge of the bed.

"So, when did Jesse leave?"

"Four days ago," I mumble.

"To Maryland?"

"Yeah."

"Same town you grew up in?"

"No. I grew up in Annapolis. His family lives in Chestertown."

"So, you guys are...?"

I shake my head. "He needs to take care of some family stuff. He'll be back."

"When?"

I avoid his gaze. "Soon."

"When's his return ticket for?"

I bite my lip. "He and I have an agreement."

"That you wait around for him indefinitely...?"

"It's not like that."

Now he looks annoyed. "I thought things were done."

I can't find any good way to respond. "Um, well..."

His face tenses up. He looks away, then looks at me. "Adam. I like you. A lot. I can't stand it to see Jesse hurt you. But don't jerk me around. If it's not really over with him, then I should probably go." He stands up. "I don't want to make this situation worse for you—"

I stand up too, completely surprised by my own actions. My heart is racing and everything's a blur. I pull Kevin close, and I kiss him. He wraps his arms around me, under my t-shirt, up my back. I run my hands down, over his shorts, feeling his butt, then up to his head where I run my fingers through that thick, curly hair of his.

A testosterone haze fuels a hallucinatory ecstasy.

Time slows down then ceases to exist for me entirely. He and I are shirtless, then in bed. Soon we are both naked. He's bigger than I thought he'd be, or perhaps he's just engorged because he's as horny as I am.

"Let me get something," I whisper as he runs his tongue down my neck, and I shiver.

"Sure," he says. "I'll be right here."

I get up off the bed, head down the hall, and it's only as I put my hand on the bathroom door that reality shatters my euphoric bliss. My knees actually give out a bit. What have I done? What am I about to do? Oh god. No. No no no.

Yes?

I hurry into the bathroom, careful to avoid looking at the mirror. I stumble over the pen and the pad of paper to the chest of drawers. I pull open the bottom drawer, and there they are, little square wrappers lying amidst big white cloth sock spheres. I pick one up a condom and turn it over in my fingers.

Can I really do this? Can I really destroy the most beautiful thing in my life?

And then I think of all the emails unanswered, all the calls unanswered, all the text messages unanswered, all the requests to raid in Jesse's favorite game that have gone ignored, how the most beautiful thing in my life has somehow morphed into desolate, lonely, silent suffering, a suffering that no one understands because I am living in Florida and going to school for the thing I have always wanted to study.

I palm the condom, turn, and make the mistake of letting my gaze stray across the mirror. My reflection is pounding his fists into his mirror, shrieking, albeit silently from my perspective, at the top of his lungs.

I gulp and walk to the mirror. My reflection pants and holds up his cell. "Stop!"

I throw down the condom and pick up the pad and paper. "Isn't this what you wanted?"

"You're doing it wrong. Keep going and you'll wreck things with Kevin and hate yourself forever. Listen. You need to end it with Jesse—"

New text follows on his cell phone, but I'm already writing out a response. "I fucking love Jesse! Why can't anyone understand that? I fucking LOVE HIM." I slam the pad into the mirror.

My reflection moves the cell phone so my paper isn't covering it up. "Fine. I understand. You're in love. Peachy. Does he love you? Does someone who loves you ignore you while making you feel ashamed for wanting attention from someone else?"

He pushes the phone at the mirror with an expression of total exasperation on his face. My face. It's my face staring back at me, I realize. My face is telling me these things. The way he's looking at me now, I don't think he's ever appeared more disappointed. And he's about to really let go. I recognize that expression he's making. That's the face I make when I'm about to really lay into someone because their behavior has completely run the limits of my patience.

"Jesse never loved you," my reflection's cell phone says. "He was always just using you to feel good about himself. Jesse doesn't love you now and he never did!"

I shriek and hurl my fists into the glass. Everything is red. My vision is red. And then I realize there's blood and broken glass has filled the sink and covered the floor, and I can't feel anything past my wrists, and my blood is everywhere.

There's a person against me, too, and I'm sobbing, but Kevin's here now and he's holding me in his arms. We're sitting on the floor, on the bath mat, his back against the bathtub and my back against his chest.

"Hey. It's okay." He's gripping my elbows with his hands. "You're gonna be okay."

I sob, and I'm utterly naked, sitting here covered in my own blood, bleeding more onto myself, but Kevin's voice is like a beacon cutting through the fog. "It'll be okay," he says, and I believe him, somehow.

Later, there are sounds of him rummaging through the medicine cabinet, or what's left of it, and I realize my back is against the bathtub. Then he's holding me again, and there's a stinging—hydrogen peroxide on my fingers and hands. "Still got all your digits," he says. "Don't worry." They're red and black, though, and they sting where he touches them with gauze.

I find my hands covered with white cloth bandages. Feeling has returned, and I wish for them to be numb again, because they're on fire. Kevin's got my broom and dustpan and he's cleaning up shards of broken glass wearing nothing but a pair of Tommy Hilfiger boxer briefs and his shoes. I'd laugh if it wasn't both sweet and my fault that he's doing this. I look at the mirror, which is the front part of the medicine cabinet. It's off one hinge and the reflective part is mutilated. It looks like maybe it's reflecting bits and pieces here and there, but not enough to see anything clearly.

I gulp. "You don't have to do this."

"Don't worry about it," Kevin says.

"What time is it?"

"About seven."

"Aren't you missing work?"

"I called them already."

"What'd you tell them?"

"That someone really important to me is in serious trouble, and I'm helping him out."

"You really don't have—" I try to push myself to a stance, but the pain in my hands flares. "Ow!"

"Take it easy."

Later he helps to the couch, and he puts his arm around me. I lie into his side, and he lies into mine.

"Someone hurt me really bad once," Kevin says.

"Yeah?"

"I thought no one could possibly understand how I felt." He smirks. "But this shit happens all the time. Gay or straight. Doesn't matter. People walk on each other's emotions. But you know what makes it worth it for me?"

"What?"

"Moments like this." He kisses my head.

I look down at my cloth wrapped hands, and I shake my head. Everything still feels hazy.

Kevin turns so we're looking at each other. "So, I want to ask…"

"Sure." I figure it's not possible for me to mess this up any worse than I already have. "Ask away."

"It seems like… you didn't like what you saw in the mirror."

"Yeah. You could say that."

He nods. "Sorry I let us rush things."

"No, really, it's not your fault—"

He holds up a hand. "No more rushing."

"Okay." I close my eyes and let my head fall onto his chest.

When I open my eyes again, I am horizontal, and I realize with a start I'm lying in bed. I fumble for my cell phone—3 am—and still no reply from Jesse to the plea for help my reflection sent yesterday. Kevin lies on the couch underneath the extra blanket I keep in the bathroom. He's on his back, his chest rising and falling gently, as adorable as ever.

I get up out of bed, and I'm surprised to feel the cloth bandages wrapped around my hands. The shock is momentary, then yesterday evening comes flooding back to me. I look over Kevin and spot the broom leaning against the wall next to the trash can. Kevin's and my clothes are still strewn across the floor.

I use the bathroom, then move to wash my hands, but then realize that's probably not the best idea with all these bandages. I face the broken medicine cabinet momentarily. There's no reflection anymore, just Tylenol, hydrogen peroxide, sunscreen, and a bag of cotton balls that now looks a lot emptier than I remember it being.

Back in the main room, I turn on the small desk lamp beside my computer. Despite the anti-reflective coating, I can see my dim reflection in the monitor. He's following my motions now, and matching my facial expressions too.

He always used to know what I was thinking. Perhaps he's angry about what I did in the bathroom. I can't say I blame him. Who's this guy looking back at me now, I wonder? I'm not very certain. But at least he doesn't look disappointed with me anymore.

Chaos and Fear

My father grew up in inner city Chicago. This was in the 1960's, when the white population had fully evacuated into the suburbs, where they wouldn't have lived near Blacks, Hispanics, and the descendants of Italian immigrants—men like my father. By the late 1990's, as a new generation came of working age, one that was significantly less racist than their parents, young, well-to-do white people flocked back into the city seeking lower rent. The influx continued throughout the aughts, and today large portions of the inner city have been thoroughly gentrified.

But that was not the case when I was born in the early 1980's. My father wanted me growing up in a rural area not just because it was safer. He wanted me isolated from a culture that would teach me to think of myself as inferior because of my genetic lineage. Racism thrives as much in the minds of its victims as its perpetrators.

In large part, his plan worked. Rural racists lacked the framework for categorizing any non-white groups besides Blacks, Hispanics, and Asians. Since my mother's family is all English and Irish, my skin tone is lighter than my father's, and so I got to be considered "white." This put me in a somewhat ridiculous situation as a child, one in which my classmates insisted that I was white, while my extended family insisted I wasn't. I can't say I've ever experienced racism in my own country, and I was certainly never afraid for my safety over it.

But still I knew fear.

It is hard to describe the state of mind that a gay individual must achieve in such an environment. Things that come naturally to one's peers—flirting, notes to your crushes, admissions to friends of one's desires—all of it must be suppressed, and each thought, each and every moment of truly *feeling* comes accompanied with paralyzing fear, and a boat load of shame to boot. "What will happen if someone finds me out?" I, admittedly, took the path of least resistance. Until I was in college, my policy was simply that no one must ever know.

There was also visceral fear.

A friend and I were walking home one night from his house to my house. We were used to cutting through a particular alley into my back yard, because it was faster. We'd done that many times over the years. And one night, in a town of only ten thousand surrounded by corn fields for hundreds of miles on all sides, we accidentally stumbled past a drug deal–in the alley behind my own house.

We realized what we were walking past far too late. My friend urged me to run, but I insisted on playing it cool until we'd reached my garage. He tugged at my sleeve and said one of the dealers was following us. I insisted we walk calmly. I didn't look back.

When we finally did reach my garage, we ran as fast as we could for my house. That was immediate, visceral, life-in-danger fear. In those moments, I could not have told you whether I would be safe and sound in the days and months that followed. It was an existential dread far more intense and gut-curdling than any social ostracism I might have been suffering. A man with sinister intent may have been immediately at my back.

We made it back to my house, but I remember sitting in my room, solemn for many minutes, unable to play whatever video game it was we had wanted to play. My friend encouraged me to move past my funk, but I needed time to settle into my new reality, for that is what bouts of such sudden and complete fear do, they create a new reality. They break down old perceptions of natural order and create new ones. I never walked home through that alley at night again. I even avoided it during the day for a time.

The stories in this section all deal with fear and the existential chaos that results. In *The Blazrath*, the fear has passed and the characters are now struggling to grapple with their new reality. However, *The Abcontinuum* and *Bastards* show that sometimes there is no easy escape. There is not always a stable reality waiting on the other side—the crisis has no "after." *The Keyhole* takes this a step further by suggesting that overcoming fear might be a perpetual process, one we are doomed to repeat endlessly throughout our lives as new challenges present themselves.

Fear need not rule us. I eventually threw off the shackles of the culture that taught me homophobic fear of myself. I decided not to live by twisted, unjust rules. I hope that these stories, as well as others in this vain I have yet to write, will help my readers to be better at staring down fear and challenging the foundations of its existence.

Bastards

Bastards.

All of them.

Filthy, stinking, treacherous—

Bastards.

I would kill them all if I could. I could use a knife. Guns are too simple. Though something like an assault rifle or bazooka would be fun. But I'm a simple guy. Maybe just a crowbar. Or perhaps I could get more exotic. Some kind of infection that would induce liquefaction. That could be enjoyable. I'd have to be careful not to infect myself, though.

Bastards.

I pull my legs, one over the other, through the muck and I can see waves of bright green gas rising up off the surface of the greenish-gray-brown gunk that comes up to my waist. My ears ring and the world is wobbling, but—

Bastards.

All of them.

I told them. I told them so many times.

Ben was the worst. Always shooting down my ideas. No matter what ingenious design scheme I'd come up with, no matter how clever my implementation was, Ben would find a way to shoot it down and suggest something stupid instead. Always ignoring my suggestions. Pathetic and stupid. The worst of them. A ship full of idiots and only me to keep them going. But the joke is on them. That ship won't be spaceworthy for long without me.

Bastards.

The vines—ropes of green before my eyes, hanging down from branches gnarled with flaky bark—spin a bit too hard to my left, and I nearly lose my balance. I stabilize just in time. I won't land in this gunk. Inhaling it is bad, and I don't want to think about what will happen if it gets anywhere near my mouth or nose. The fumes waft up from everywhere, though, and there's a bitter taste in the back of my throat, like a bad aftertaste, like I accidentally let a drop of dandruff shampoo hit my tongue and even after rinsing it really good that damn disgusting taste lingers. Except this is all over, seeping into me, poisoning me slowly.

I would have killed faster, given the chance.

But now the joke's on them. They won't run the ship without me. Any minute now, I'm going to hear a roar and a crash and violent explosion. It will resound from beyond the ropey vines and curtains of leaves above my head. I will feel a quaking in the ground and perhaps even a shockwave as the engine core sets off a massive explosion. I imagine Ben and Cynthia and Kylie all melting and screaming in agony.

Bastards.

Kylie was the worst, actually. I know she went behind my back. I know it. She was the viper pretending to be a pussy cat. Always listening, always saying kind things, and then when push came to shove, I saw her glowering at me from the door of the ship. She saw me and she pushed the button to retract the causeway.

And they all left.

I hate them all so much.

I wish I could stomp, but the swamp gunk makes it hard to move my legs. Every step is torture, an enormous expenditure of energy, energy that should be fueling my vast intellect, intellect which should be keeping their ship in one piece. It will all fall to pieces now. It will.

Without me they are doomed.

Bastards.

They deserve it.

I pull my right leg up, and it is all I can do to keep my balance, and I am so close. I put my foot down, and now the gunk only comes up to my hips. With my next beleaguered step, it is at my knees. The knoll in the swamp is spinning, but it lies in my vision before me, shrouded in a hazy green mist.

They will regret leaving me, Cynthia most of all. The English language does not have words vile enough to describe her. She is stupid beyond belief for the position she occupies. They never should have put her in charge of engineering on that ship. Never. Always using "being nice" as an excuse to shut me up, always using "my outbursts" against me when they were all completely justified. I wouldn't have to get so angry if everyone around me wasn't always fucking things up with their incompetence. And that stupid counselor she made me see. What was his name? Gary. I've never met a stupider and more inept person than Gary. How the hell is someone who obviously has issues supposed to "help" someone like me who has none?

Besides being betrayed, of course. That's an issue if there ever was one.

Bastards.

I'm on my back now. Not sure how I got there. But I'm on the knoll. It's solid ground against my back, not swamp muck, though I can still smell the reek. It permeates everything. The vines above me are spinning a full three hundred and sixty degrees, and I suspect some of the vines in my vision are duplicates of the same vine. The trees and flowers, the chirps and squawks are almost—

Bastards.

I'll hear the explosion any minute now. Any minute now, they'll all die. They deserve this so much more than I do.

They actually left me. And they knew. I'm sure they knew. And all because I tried to help them. They're just jealous of my superior intellect. That's always how it's been, hasn't it? Even though humanity needs to control its colossal and complex technological infrastructure, even though they need us, the incompetent and mediocre will always lash out. It's because of their inferiority complex.

They can't stand that we're so much better than them.

They're bastards.

Any minute now, I'll hear the crash and feel the shockwave. And I'll be able to imagine them all burning and screaming and dying. I hope they are thrown far enough from the engine room so that they are not vaporized instantly. I want them to wreathe and suffer and die in agony. And melt. I will imagine them melting. I'm imagining it now and it feels so good.

They won't die quietly and painlessly, in some hallucinatory sleep induced by swamp fumes.

Bastards.

I imagine them burning and screaming in pain, and my eyes slide closed, and even the blackness behind my eyelids is spinning.

They'll pay for this. They'll pay.

Any minute now.

It will all be over for them. They'll see.

I'll be alive, and they'll be dead.

They'll see.

The Abcontinuum

"Well," Kayla muttered. "*That* wasn't quite what I expected."

"What did you expect?" a voice beside her said.

Kayla jolted at the sound of the unexpected voice. She turned to witness a whorl of indigo and fuchsia, which had formerly been a warped brick wall, as it finished coalescing into the body of a man. His skin shone neon-green and his eyes radiated blue headlight beams.

"I expected the abcontinuum to remain inside its chamber."

The man turned up one edge of his glowing lips, chortled, trained his blue headlights on her, and shrugged morosely. "Looks like it didn't."

His body congealed into brown flotsam and drifted away, dispersing in all directions. Even down and up.

The floor and ceiling of the laboratory had disappeared.

Raw terror ate at her gut. Beads of sweat dripped off her forehead, and she stretched her fingers. She wanted to reach out, but her arms remained glued to her sides.

Her eyes darted about, searching for some remaining assemblage of her laboratory, but it had all gone. The abcontinuity chamber had been the first to dissolve. It had become a sea of pink cotton candy. The floors and wall had given away next to crimson jellyfish, followed by every furnishing and apparatus going up in a puff of smoke, then the smoke turned to water and the water to ice, then it was on to dirty jello.

Presently, a stampede of paper of cups was busy roiling into stardust on her left and an army of yellow insects the size of Kayla's head on her right.

Kayla gulped.

"What would you say—" The man had reappeared, though now his skin was deep black and he wore glasses. "—if I told you that the abcontinuum has always been your reality and you were just blind to it?"

Kayla jerked her gaze toward him. His head was expanding like a balloon. She took a few deep breaths and sputtered, "That's ridiculous."

He grinned manically and shrugged as his head floated up off his body and away. "What's ridiculous in one context can be sensical in another. It seems you're not making the connection. You've missed the obvious conclusion—" His voiced drifted up and away and became inaudible. His body melted into ochre jelly, then sprouted limbs, like a tree, and branched, the branches sprouting golden butterflies. The shimmering insects leapt toward Kayla, and she flinched, but they only trailed golden dust before being absorbed into a chorus of ringing handbells.

Kayla closed her eyes.

Think, Kayla. Abcontinuity is powered by an anti-material electromagnetic field. It couldn't possibly have breached the chamber. Something else is going on.

But she didn't like any of the other possibilities. The first that jumped to her mind was that she was crazy.

I'm not crazy... am I? If you can ask yourself the question, you're not, right?

She wasn't really sure.

"Kayla?" A familiar voice.

Kayla turned, leapt on instinct. "David!"

Her eyes met his warm smile. She grabbed his arm and squeezed.

"What happened, Kayla?"

"I started up the abcontinuity engine for another test run, and then... all this..." She cast her free arm up to the herd of ruddy amphibians swimming over their heads and the growth of blue algae melting beside them.

He shot her a queer look. "And... what?"

"The..." Kayla stuttered, winced. Disillusionment and putrid rejection joined terror in her mix of emotional miasma. "It's all... don't you see—?"

"Kayla." David's face turned stern and he took a step toward her, reached out. "Why don't you come with me? Everything's going to be all ri— all ri— all ri—" His whole body stuttered and crackled like a skipping record in three dimensions, then he burst into grey confetti and flittered away.

Tears streamed down Kayla's face.

"The abcontinuum is reality," the man said.

Kayla twisted her whole body, lashed out with her hands, her fingers claws. "Shut up!" His body rippled like water as her hands passed uselessly through him.

"If you like." The man sank downward, falling through a floor of roses.

"Why?" Kayla whispered.

"No particular reason." The man stood on her other side now, from the direction of his voice. Something gurgled behind him.

"Why me?" She shook all over, huddled on the ground.

"No reason for that either." His voice sounded from below.

"Take me back," she pleaded.

"There is no back from here." From above.

"Reality! I want reality back! Like it was before!"

His voice affected sadness, right in front of her. "It's always been this way. You just couldn't see it until now."

"How do I unsee it?" She huddled herself on the ground, eyes clenched shut.

The sound of drifting, shuffling papers from all around, and then, "you still don't understand."

Kayla huffed and panted and bawled.

Make this stop. Make it stop. Make it stop.

"Honey?"

Kayla shot to a stance, albeit shakily. "Mom?"

Her mother's eyes watered and she wrung her right wrist with her left hand. "Oh, my darling girl."

Still afraid of what this next vision would bring, she shot forward anyway, wrapped her arms around that familiar blue sweater, put her head on the maternal shoulder and cried.

"My darling girl," her mom said. "You'll be all right."

"Can you make it stop, mom?" Kayla bawled.

"No, I'm sorry, honey. I can't. No one can."

Kayla bawled harder.

"I'm so scared, mom."

"You've always been strong. You'll make it through."

Kayla sniffed. "I'll try."

When her mother said nothing for a time, Kayla decided to look up. Her mother's features had hardened. No, she was literally immobile. All at once, Kayla realized that her whole body was turning the color of granite. It darkened to coal and adopted a similar texture. Her body grew hot, and Kayla had to release her, bawling anew.

The statue of her mother erupted into flames, then the flames turned green and became bubbles, floating away, popping, forming knots and twists of goop.

Kayla bit her lip.

"Yes?" the man asked.

"I didn't ask for you," Kayla's fear had turned hard.

"I know."

"This is all that's left?"

The man didn't respond, so Kayla turned to face him. He was nodding.

"What do I do now?"

"Nothing," the man said. "Everything, and nothing at all."

The Keyhole

NOVEMBER 1

Lost the antechamber today. Library, kitchen, bedroom, bathroom and corridor to Exit remain. I fear losing the library. Would really set us back. V says she's more worried about the kitchen. Doesn't want to starve. I reminded her that we only have five rooms left and it takes more than five days to starve to death.

I linked into Exit again. Threw everything I had in way of decryption at it. Nothing. Didn't even so much as give up a byte in response. Stuck with brute force hacking, which will take too long. Exit hummed a bit, but that's just the locking mechanism taunting us. Will try coding up something tonight. V is distributing food and water from the kitchen to the other four rooms.

NOVEMBER 2

As I feared, it was the library. V is going to the bathroom every ten minutes. I told her that would not affect her bladder after the bathroom's disappearance. She is worried it will be next. I asked if she was going to redistribute the toilet, too.

Link to Exit is still producing nil. I can modulate the tones of its humming, but that's it. Still no movement, and its little gears and levers haven't budged one bit. I can see light through the tiny hole at its center. Escape is so close.

Will discuss logistics with V tonight. We need to change our strategy.

NOVEMBER 3

We awoke to a klaxon and had to scramble out of the bedroom. I lost my notebook, but was thankfully able to grab up my computer and journal. Was smart to keep them under my pillow.

We are left with kitchen, bathroom, and corridor. Will start sleeping in the corridor, as that will be the last to go. I do not feel close to unlocking its secret, but I pretend to for V's sake. She has taken to tapping at random controls on Exit. I told her the computer is doing the same thing much faster, but she persists.

NOVEMBER 4

No more kitchen. Just bathroom off the corridor. V locked herself in the bathroom, and when I realized what she had done, I had to shout at her to come out. She's in such a state. I don't know why they put children in here. I mean, me, sure, I've had most my life, but V is so innocent. It kills me. But we do what we must.

V asked how long it would take to try all the combinations with the computer. I told her how many millennia and she frowned. I worried she would run back into the bathroom, but she didn't.

NOVEMBER 5
V took to pacing the corridor. I do not blame her. She must be so distraught. Or she just needs to use the bathroom, which is now gone.

I am going to minimize writing time today. If there is no entry tomorrow, well dear reader, you will know what became of V and myself.

NOVEMBER 7
We had huddled in the corner near Exit. My computer sat, still churning through its countless permutations, Exit emitting its tonal hums. The clock ticked ever closer to midnight, and V was asking me questions about death that I was ignoring.

Suddenly, she looked at the pinhole of light, small but radiant in the darkness, and said, "what if we've been thinking about it wrong?"

She stood, walked up to Exit, and put both pinky fingers in the keyhole, then pulled. The mechanisms of Exit simply fell away around her hands—the hole grew wider.

Corridor rumbled. I jumped to my feet and ran to her side. She grasped the chasm with both her hands and wrenched it wider. Now able to help, I grabbed one side and she the other. Gears, levers, buttons, diodes, and all components of Exit fell away under our combined strength. Corridor flooded red and rumbled. I grabbed up the journal, abandoning my meager bed and food and water remains. I pushed V through the keyhole, now as big as a door, and clambered through myself. Corridor dissolved behind us, and the remains of Exit fell away, too.

I sit now writing this before a new Exit. This one doesn't have a keyhole, only a vidpanel displaying the world beyond it. And there are only fifteen rooms in our new arena, giving barely more than two weeks. It will be quite a challenge. V is smiling though. She thinks we can take this one, too.

The Blazrath

You wouldn't believe what
just happened.

What?

That blazrath showed up.

?!

Uh huh.

No way. What did it want?

I don't know. It just came in,

sat down in front of me and started spewing bile all over the place. Brad was with me though. I think I avoided the worst of it because he was here. You know the blazraths. They're less antagonistic if you're with others.

                              Did you get a sample, at
                                              least?

Yeah. Computer's going over it now. Some arsenic, aluminum, lead. Heavy on lead this time. Acidity was through the roof. Lots of vitriol.

                              What did you say to it?

Oh, just the usual, I guess. My heart was pounding out of my chest.

                              I'll bet! Are you sure it was
                                              the one?

Yeah. Definitely.

154

But it's been so long since
you've seen it.

It was definitely the one. I'd
recognize it anywhere. The
thing was stalking me for
over a year.

How did it seem?

Agitated. Annoyed. Proba-
bly hurt. You know what we
found out about them,
right?

You mean that report Julie
wrote?

Yeah.

I haven't read it yet. What'd
she find out?

Well, we thought that they
just saw us as food, like
predator and prey. But it's
more complicated than that.
They think of the flaying
and dicing and devouring as
some kind of morbid eternal
union.

Wait wait wait.

Do you mean to tell me that
the blazraths think of that
as some kind of twisted
marriage?

That's what Julie thinks.

Wow.

You're going to be careful
coming home, right? Is Ben
going with you?

No. But I asked Mark, and
he's going the same way.

I'll be fine.

Be extra careful. And let me
know if the computer says
anything about the bile
sample.

You weren't exposed, I
hope?

No. Brad put up that forcefield around both of us right

away. And I'm glad he did. I
was just sort of stunned.

It was spewing that stuff everywhere. Probably covered
half the cafeteria. Wrecked
the doors and the front wall,
too.

                    Wait. It came indoors?

Yeah!

                              Weird!

                    Just barged right inside?

Yup.

                    They never do that.

This one did. Everyone put
up their personal forcefields
right away.

                    Oh my. James, I think this
                    one had a real crush on you.
                    Maybe even its form of love.

It wanted to cook me, tear

off my skin, dice my muscles,
and drink my blood.

You said it yourself. That's
love to them.

It went away, right?

Yeah, it left all in a huff, just
like how it arrived.

Wow. Kepler-186f's first in-
terspecies heartbreak. Mind
if I write a research paper on
this?

Yes. I do.

Pretty please?

Absolutely not.

Okay, fine. But if I fail out of
grad school, I'm blaming
you.

Won't happen. You're too
smart.

You know what they say

about flattery.

"Beware the pheromonic
bile of a blazrath for it will
melt your skin as well as
your heart?"

Very funny, Mr. English major.

Seriously, I want you being
extra careful on the way
home.

I will.

You promise?

Scout's honor.

See you soon.

Love you.

Love you, too.

Society

It is my prediction that going forward, there will be two major themes that dominate my work. The first of these is an exploration of what it means to have "society."

Margaret Thatcher famously declared there to be no such thing. This stance has become the touchstone of neoliberal thought. Especially in an age when eight billion human beings inhabit the Earth and each of our livelihoods is bound up in an globally expansive economic bureaucracy, it can be comforting to conceive of ourselves as entirely atomic and self-reliant individuals. But I believe it is damaging to hold this opinion. We can see the extent of such damage in the 2016 United States presidential election results. One way to view the ascendancy of Trump on a pan-cultural scale is as the end result of the ideology of unchecked selfishness and narcissism. Or, even more frighteningly, perhaps the *beginning* of our problems rather than the end.

So then, even if we are headed in the direction of anti-society, what then does it mean to have society, so as to one day hopefully regain it?

The brief answer is that society occurs wherever two groups with different, even competing, needs and wants can arrive at mutually agreed-upon rules that safeguard the continued existence of both sides. This can happen on the scale of two individuals, as it does in *Meerkat and Lynx*, but as more than two competing actors arrive on the scene, the agreements get expanded, then later codified as laws, and soon we end up with governmental bureaucracy, which neoconservatives hate because of the threat it represents to individual autonomy, but I would argue that there is no such thing as pure autonomy, and we must instead build the system whose price for maintaining freedom, liberty, and justice is one we can afford to pay, now and over the long term.

Inevitably, in groups of expanding complexity, questions arise about the correct establishment of authority, a topic explored in *Halls of Power*. We must also figure out how to deal with the people who will insist on breaking the social contract, and the possibility that mightier but less benevolent groups (read: either "invaders" or "assholes;" take your pick) will break our social contracts for us. Such dangers are highlighted in *Temple of the Setting Sun* and *We Were Here First*.

And then there is the era-spanning exploration of social development, which I took my first stab at in *Lunar Eclipse*. My readers told me that it reminded them of

Isaac Asimov's *Foundation*, which I had not read before penning my story, but did in fact find my way to in 2016.

Society most certainly does exist. To insist on pure individualism is to end up in a society of either mob rule or anarchy, and both of those configurations produce enough injustice and oppression as to be unsatisfactory for the majority of their constituents.

As we go forward, we must find ways of living and working together that safeguard and provide for us all. We will have to change how we think about ourselves and our place in the world. Science fiction, I would argue, is the literary mode best equipped to tackle such a daunting task.

Meerkat and Lynx

Meerkat pulled away a tiny, gnarled branch.

"Who's there?" he called out. He tightened his grip on his burlap fruit sack, the rough fabric digging into his other paw.

The leafless brambles across the glen shuddered, then went silent. An eerie blue glow cast long shadows out from the spot, radiating outward, barely visible under the light of the full moon.

Meerkat gulped. "I-I said who's— there?"

No, he'd done that all wrong. He should have steeled himself first. Hunter Leader was always reminding him of that. He liked to remind Meerkat that he was weak in front of the other meerkats.

Stupid.

The brambles shuddered again. The glow stuttered

and shifted. Something big shuffled across the dirt.

A burly, stout, furry face emerged from the brambles.

"Whose territory is this?" the lynx asked.

Meerkat gazed, stupefied. He truly wasn't sure. The glen was scentless. The nearby burbling river led to meerkatdom, that was for sure, but the ground here was rockier, pitted, the grass browner, and the trees, what few there were, short and gnarled. Almost as though he were coming upon lynxdom.

But the air was empty. No wind, either. The only sound was the burbling brook.

Meerkat decided to steel himself after all. "Do you wish to claim this place for lynxdom?"

The lynx strode out of the brambles fully on four paws. His soft, white fur glistened in the moonlight. "I should." He strode carefully, purposefully. "What about you?"

A basket sat atop the lynx's back, its sides composed of dried, translucent reeds. The reeds stretched from the sides of the basket, wrapping around his stomach. Within it lay dozens of glowing berries, the source of the blue light that glided smoothly alongside its bearer.

Meerkat shook his head vigorously, then reminded himself to be strong. "I suppose I might. Unless... will you claim the grove?"

"We shall both leave this glen," the lynx said resolutely. He was an impressive creature. Probably as much muscle in his hind legs as Meerkat had in his whole body. "And it shall be claimed by neither side. At least not this evening. Do we have a deal?"

Meerkat nodded vigorously.

Lynx folded his ears back suddenly and sniffed the

air. "What is that?"

Meerkat sniffed. "I smell nothing."

"Not territory scent, but..." Lynx turned his head one way, then another, still working his nose muscles. He frowned, perplexed. He took a careful step toward Meerkat, sniffed again, and his eyes widened. "What do you have in that sack?"

Meerkat tightened his grip on the sack, the rough burlap grating against his paws. "Nothing! It's nothing."

Lynx dared another few steps closer. "It smells delicious! Tell me what it is."

"Elderberries only." Meerkat dared to point a finger up at Lynx's basket. "You've got berries, too." He felt stupid the moment he said it.

Lynx snorted and let out an annoyed hiss. "These taste like dust. But our glowberry loupes keep the Charnel out of our caves."

Meerkat's eyes widened. "You can keep the Charnel away?"

"You can't?" Lynx twitched his right whiskers.

"And you've never had an elderberry?"

Lynx's pupils narrowed. "... No."

"We can run fast and fight hard." Meerkat felt taller and stronger just saying the words. "But the Charnel catch some of us. Going home... well, I'd feel better if I could strap a glowberry to my back."

Lynx's stomach grumbled audibly, and his jaw quirked. "Are you proposing a trade?"

Meerkat puffed out his chest. "Yes."

"Deal," Lynx said. He shook himself, and the glow wobbled and jostled. A berry finally fell, plopping to the ground at his side.

Meerkat retrieved an elderberry from his sack, and held it forward. Lynx took it in his paw, and Meerkat scooped up the glowberry. Its skin was translucent, and the glow oozed out of the fruity insides speckled with dark black seeds.

"Mmmm..." Lynx gnashed audibly, snarfing as he inhaled the elderberry. Purple juice stained the short furs about his maw.

Meerkat held the glowberry above his head, basking in its luminance. "How long does it last?" he asked.

Lynx licked his teeth. "Four days from the time it was picked. I nabbed this one at noon."

Meerkat smiled. An idea hatched, unfolding within his mind. Fear struck, but he pushed it aside. He could show Hunter Leader he was wrong! This was his chance!

"Lynx?" Meerkat tried. "Would you like to trade more elderberries? Our territory has no glowberries."

Lynx nodded. "They only grow in the mountains. And we have no elderberries there." He stood and stared, his face impassive, his eyes glowing like the berries on his back.

Meerkat's heart fell. Maybe Lynx would attack and take all his elderberries, wound him, or worse.

"Come back in two moons," Lynx said. "I will bring two others, each of us with a glowberry basket. Bring two more of your kind, and three sacks of those."

"Deal."

Lynx smiled a friendly smile, and with a nod, turned and loped off into the brambles, beyond, up the river and toward his mountain home. The blue aura followed him, except for the light from the glowberry that Meerkat held at his side.

Meerkat grinned and took off in the other direction, away downstream, toward his own home, already planning his next conversation with Hunter Leader.

Halls of Power

My heart beats out a triumphant rhythm. My face is sweat-streaked, I breathe in and out, long, deep draws. I am covered in dirt, grit, gravel, slime, mucus, and other substances too wretched to mention. Here I am. I succeeded. My name will be etched in light atop the Presidum, I have earned the right to lead.

And here it is. Finally. I stand before the door.

I was told it would be made of wood, but I didn't imagine it would be quite so rustic. It's quite a contrast to the pits, chasms, mires, saw chambers, locust nests, and other horrors that lie behind me. Worst was the chamber of predatory nanorobots. Lost the last of my EM grenades to them. Made the cybernetic lizards more difficult to deal with.

I remind myself that I am here. It is over, and I am at

the door. Intact. I turn my hands over a few times, just to make sure of that. I scan the rock ridge around the door too, just in case there's final booby trap, but neither my eyes nor my computer pad find anything.

I raise my hand steadily. One more deep breath, and I knock, three times, rhythmically.

Steps from within, growing closer.

The door swings open.

A man appears. Younger than I expected.

I beam at him.

He scowls, then he scoffs, then he turns and wanders inward, leaving the door ajar.

"Chraz?" I call after him. "Chraz Ovan?"

I push the door open a bit further, and a room appears. The room is carpeted. A hearth bathes the room in a dull glow. Candles sit atop a wooden table, and there's another wooden door against the far wall. Chraz throws himself into a reclining chair by the fireplace; his back is to me. He props his feet up on an ottoman and releases an audible sigh.

I clear my throat, but Chraz does not speak or move.

"May I come in?" I try.

His voice is weary, sounding older than his outward appearance. "The sooner the better. That's an awful draft."

I step inside and close the door. Still, Chraz does not move or speak.

I shuffle from foot to foot and struggle to reclaim the confidence I had possessed just moments ago. Suspicion wells up within me. Perhaps it was a holographic illusion and the Path of Calamity hasn't actually ended; this could be some new trial disguised as the finish line.

"Haven't I succeeded?"

"You have."

"You're Chraz?"

"I am."

My eyes dart about his room. The fireplace is your stand brickwork affair. The sofa chair and ottoman are green felt with little silver studs lining the edges. The walls are covered in red wallpaper, and packed book-shelves line two sides of the room. The fireplace is against one other, and the fourth wall is covered in framed photographs, pictures of all our high ministers.

None of the interior appears even remotely hostile, nor are there any off-putting minor details that might harbor a concealed danger. I take a few careful steps to-wards where Chraz sits. "Then I've won?"

"Yes."

"I await certification."

Chraz releases another long sigh. "You won't like it."

I swallow hard and compress all my facial muscles. A younger me might have raised my voice, but I keep my voice steady and firm, and my volume low. "I have braved temperatures, toxins, genetically and cybernet-ically modified animals, and overcome five kilometers of other horrors. The rules you established were quite clear. I insist on claiming my certificate without further delay!"

Chraz stands, turns and looks harshly into my eyes. "Why do we have certification?"

I am unfazed. I have braved far worse than conde-scension. "To protect the truth."

"And why does it need protecting?"

"It would be dangerous in unskilled hands. We make

sure only the best gain access so that it is handled responsibly. That's why the Path of Calamity exists, and why you and our forefathers wrote the Establishment of Authority."

Chraz pinches the bridge of his nose, closes his eyes, nods a few times, releases another long sigh, and pulls himself wearily across the gorgeous carpeting toward the wall. He doesn't need to say anything. I imagine him thinking something along the lines of, 'They're still teaching them that shit.'

He taps at a recession in a large log support built into the wall and a screen shimmers into existence over the rustic logs. "8.4 percent of participants fail at the precipice. 10.2 percent of participants fail to cross the bog-of-many-poisons. 12.7 percent lose to the nanite chamber. 2.3 percent flunk the chamber of extreme temperatures..." Here Chraz turns to look at me. "You know I petitioned them to leave that one out? 'Extreme temperatures?!' I said. 'Do you really think that the candidates will bring a small arsenal, survival gear, and every antidote in existence, but forget a bloody jacket?' Well, 2.3 percent, so go figure. 7.1 percent fail to pass the avalanche chasm—"

I raise a hand. "Wait. What is this?"

"Certification. Are you listening or not?"

I stride across the room until I am standing next to him and his holographic screen. I look over it. Indeed, it lists the relative ratios of candidate failures per trial. "That's it?"

"Yes."

I purse my lips. "You're telling me that the deep wisdom, the secret lore of Chraz Ovan that we only trust the most responsible, most intelligent, strongest and brightest with... that it's a list of *percentages*?"

"Yes."

I feel faint, and am simultaneously surprised, after all my training that it should be here and now, after the trial that they could invent something capable of shocking my system. I let out a small laugh and draw a hand up to my head. I rub the sweat off my face and wipe my hand on the remains of my shirt.

My eyes make their way back to Chraz. He looks at me with a wry grin and says, "I told you you wouldn't like it." He claps a hand on my shoulder. It takes all my willpower not to flinch away. "You'll be one of the better high ministers, I think."

I gulp. "What makes you say that?"

"You're upset. The ones who end up invading countries and dropping bombs are the ones who make it here and are apathetic. No twinge of idealism. That's important, I think."

My mind is still reeling. "A list of percentages..."

Chraz's eyes are stern. "Think about what it means."

"But it's supposed to be—" Chraz's grasp on my shoulder becomes a vice grip. I think about the percentages. I run it all over in my mind. "What do they add up to?" I ask.

Chraz smiles and releases my shoulder. He turns to his screen. "99.2." Then he presses at the wall and the hologram flickers away.

"How many of them died trying?" I ask.

"Not many," Chraz says. "But still."

I nod. Chraz returns to his chair and his ottoman.

"In the halls of power there are no easy answers. Others must be able to respect you and trust in your judgment, and you, in turn, must take ultimate responsibility for every failure, yours and those of your subordinates as well. You are used to that being a large number of people. It will soon be your entire country. It is important for them to think of you as someone with all the answers, but it is equally important—"

"—for me to understand that for all my strength and intellect, I don't possess any 'special knowledge.'"

"Your experience is special knowledge."

I find confidence returning. I walk to his chair, look down at him. I tip my head toward the door, the one across the room from where I entered, with a questioning expression, and he nods silently, gazing into the fireplace.

I walk to it, stand before it, take a deep breath, and put my hand on the handle. I take one more look at Chraz, but his gaze is fixed upon the fire. I breathe in and out once more, pull my shoulders back, and tug at the door handle. It swings open easily, and I step through the open portal into whatever lies beyond.

Temple of the Setting Sun

The bee dances through the air—or am I merely imposing my concept of dance upon it? The creature launches itself from a small flower of white, circular petals and glides down onto a bulbous blue tulip. At the base of its stem lie little ringlets of grass and dirt. Plants dot a field of small pebbles, each immaculately arranged. The pebbles form twisting rows that weave around and through one another across a field many tens of meters square, the whole thing punctuated by plants—a shrubbery here, a flowerbed there, a tree yonder, at the edge of my vision.

They do that on purpose. The temple compound goes on for hundreds of meters in all directions.

Little hills jut up throughout our cloister, and at sunset, we form into groups, each group to a hilltop, and we all sit cross-legged and hold our palms out toward the distant Western mountains as the setting sun begins its slow plummet behind the spires of distant stone, until we are all shrouded in darkness.

A voice sounds behind me. Startled, I turn.

"This must stop," one elder says to another.

The other elder pulls him by the arm, and they disappear into a dark frame of wood set into the side of the hill behind me. The door slams shut behind them and I flinch. The discord stabs at my soul. I close my eyes and focus all my attention on my breathing for many moments, then I open them and turn my attention back to the garden, but all at once I can hear them again! The elders' conversation grows loud—not loud enough for me to make out words, but loud enough that their muffled argument latches itself into my mind, and tugs me away from the state of being that is my task.

With an exasperated sigh, I stand, and I walk away through the garden, seeking another hill.

Just yesterday I made it to blue.

So close now.

A part of me is afraid of myself. I wrap my arms around this calm, this clarity. The world has never felt more vivid before. I have never felt more myself. Bees dance across flowers—I'm sure it's a dance—birds chirp, breezes waft over us. These things scare me, deep down, in the place I'm not supposed to reach into while I'm here. Or perhaps I'm mostly scared that I don't want to reach down there. I retract from that place, like I should, like they've trained me to, but should I really? That was the point in coming here after all.

We come here to reach toward the gods, but what would gods think of me, that I can continue, not knowing...

Yesterday, was the tenth and final day of the cycle. I was taken to the reflection pool, my seventh visit. Most don't normally advance as fast as I have. I blew through red, orange, and yellow. Green tripped me up once, but I made it through on the second attempt. And same with blue—I'd failed my first attempt at blue.

They took me through the tunnels yesterday, caves of dripping water and echoes and little pools across the cave floor, rivulets that run the stones like little rivers at my bare feet. We have to pull off our robes and wrap the cloth bulkily around our waists to traverse the caves.

At the end of a long, twisting passage with craggy walls comes a room of candles and finely polished marbled stone walls, bent in the shape of an oval. In the base of the oval lies the pool.

As you sit and stare at the pool, two elders on each side, the color of the water changes. They only let you go one hue beyond the one you reached last time.

I'll admit, I don't understand the technology that enables the pool to do what it does. In ancient times, this was outdoors. They utilized prisms, and the rite could only be performed during sunset, robbing the twilight ceremony of some of its splendor, as one initiate or another would utilize a hill for the prismaticum instead. And often prismaticums would get cancelled if more water than expected had evaporated between preparation and the event.

But now we have this underground pool, and the ritual can occur any time of day. Candlelight is a fine substitute for the sun. The fire might be smaller, but the whole room was shaped so as to amplify the light and focus it on the pool.

My memories of the prismaticum episodes later are always hazy. It's like trying to remember a dream. I sat, and I stared, and there was red, then orange, then yellow, then green, and after some struggle, which I remember even less than the rest of it, finally blue.

I made it to blue.

Wordless, unsmiling, I stood before the unnaturally blue plane of water, and the elders ushered me out of the cave and back into the caverns, where we traversed the two kilometers back to the gardens on the surface.

I remember, upon opening the wooden door, which squeaked on old hinges, being surprised at the blast of evening sun in my face. The surprise, just like my joy at making it to the next stage of prismaticum, I stuffed away into the same place I held my fear and my sorrow.

I wonder if it's actually good for a human being to do these things.

Who am I becoming? I suppose that's the point. But the elders never could have foreseen such events as those of the last three weeks.

My gaze is caught by a leaf, which detaches from its tree and falls, gently, swaying back and forth, to the lines of pebbles below. It must only take a handful of seconds, but in my mind it is longer. My perception of time itself has come under the control of my mental faculties.

I should be afraid, but I'm keeping my fear somewhere else.

Perhaps the elder who violated the Ultimate Protocol

was right. Perhaps I should give in. If an elder can, then...?

I've been interested in the Order of the Setting Sun for a very long time. My parents are both Remnaarites, but progressive and open-minded enough that they didn't feel the need to impress their religious beliefs on their only daughter. Though I'll admit, it probably helped that Remnaar and the Order share a common ancestor—Ancient Perlidian.

Remnaar has grown very... secular. It seems like a shell of a religion to me, some hollow husk that used to be grand and majestic, until the powerful engines of progress forced it to capitulate some of its power, and far from letting up, they did it again and again and again for centuries at a time.

And I'll admit that I feel a bit as though Remnaar deserved it. Elements of it were... unkind. The tenets and strictures were always better than the people enforcing them, though I suppose that's true of any religion.

I picked up a book in my library about religions of the world, and that's when I first heard of the Order. Their section of the book started with a huge, full-page color photograph taken from the mountain range behind the temple complex just as the sun was starting to dip behind the mountains. The orange-red fire of the sun flared dramatically and drowned out most of the details, but atop the hills in the sprawling garden complex, I could just make out the outlines of hands and fingers, pitch black against the coruscating flare. All the green of the garden was washed out into red.

And I knew. Before I had even read a single line, I

knew.

Remnaar had lost its connection to people, to nature, to the world. It had found ways to use computers and social networks and youth events to keep itself afloat, to keep itself popular and "relevant," whatever that meant. And I didn't like it.

But here, upon the page of this book, a single photo depicting a religion composed entirely of a solitary temple, and which had chosen to keep its beauty and potency and life and connection to nature at the expense of its own security. It lay in an alien culture thousands of miles distant from my home across huge expanses of ocean.

And yet I knew.

Reading the description of the Order only reinforced what my gut had already told me upon witnessing that picture.

I wanted to see what they saw. I wanted to feel what they felt. I wanted to sit before the pool and find out what happened after the last color of the rainbow, a moment that lay at the core of the foundation's beliefs, which few would achieve, and which no one talked about. Even the book could not tell me, for those who reached it had never spoken of it, except to say that they'd reached it, and that all other elders had confirmed their impressions.

The book could not tell me what lay there, beyond the setting sun.

And so I learned, and I went, and I joined.

Nothing else mattered.

I wonder now if that was wise, if I could have made other things matter more to me? It will undoubtedly be different when I go back. If there's still a place for me to go back to.

I knew the world would seem different after I left the Order and returned to "normal" life, but I had no idea...

Two weeks ago, they rounded up all the initiates. I remember, I was sitting in front of the pond surrounded by the circle of pruned hedges. I first knew something was amiss when the elder pruning the hedges suddenly stopped his work and scampered off. His off-kilter too-loud footfalls aggravated me, I remember. I hadn't fully subsumed annoyance and frustration yet at the time.

Just after I'd resettled my mind, an elder appeared in my vision and beckoned me to follow him. We walked away from the pool and through an opening in the hedge circle, down the path, across the bridge over the stream, then to the door in the far hill where the big conference hall was. I hadn't been inside since my initiation.

Why was he leading me here, I wondered with a jolt.

I remember struggling with all my might to suppress fear and worry. I frantically recalled all my recent behavior, searching for something that might cause my expulsion from the Order. Had I accidentally whispered during meditation? Had I mumbled in my sleep?

The elder led me through the door and into the underground temple complex, and we joined a congregation of elders and initiates, the whole Order from the looks of it, and we stood waiting.

Like the other initiates, I fidgeted and my eyes darted about. Speech was allowed here, in this one place in the temple, and nowhere else. But none of the elders spoke, and no initiate would dare such a thing.

A group of three elders got up atop the stage, and all our attention turned to them.

"Something has happened," the elder said.

Everyone tensed. Some initiates winced. To hear human speech after so much silence, so much training to reign in the communicative impulse, to only write letters, and then only to express that which could not be gestured, it reminded me of my first time going for a run after months of remaining sedentary. It hurt with all the power of forcing a weak muscle into sudden action. But that pain was soon forgotten.

"Fifty-two of our world's nations are now at war with the other seventy-six," the elder said. "The country in which our Temple resides is one of the fifty-two. If you are from one of the seventy-six, you must stay here, and we must discuss how to proceed with your education. Your visa has undoubtedly been revoked."

He stared at us blankly for many seconds. And then, as if an afterthought, added. "Also, the population of this country is half of what it was yesterday. Under the circumstances, we will respect any decision you might make with regard to your future here."

The weight of a star descended upon me, just then. Though the bombs had not fallen upon me literally, I'm sure they fell upon the hearts of every person in attendance. We all remained silent.

Papers were passed around, a list of which countries were at war with which.

My eyes scanned the paper in a bleary haze, but I found the nation of my allegiance. I was in with the seventy-six. My country was at now at war with the country of my temple, and my visa had become void.

I slept fitfully that night and awoke the next morning to a letter upon the floor before the door to my quarters, apparently slipped under the night before. I picked it up and read with bleary eyes.

As a religious institution, the Order was allowed to offer amnesty to any citizen of an enemy nation within its borders, so long as we remained within its walls. However, the Order insisted on caution. As much as they appreciated their patron nation, they would not fully vouch for its assurances that amnesty would be respected. In other words, it might be safer for me to leave at once, while everyone caught in such predicaments as I was still trying to sort themselves out.

At the same time, my host country was not the only nation that had suffered massive casualties. Bombardment had hit my country as well, apparently, though the letter could not tell me where or to what degree.

Whatever my decision, the Order would understand.

I moved through morning prayer and meditation into a very familiar daze. Meditation, surprisingly, came easy. How could it not? The sun was shining, birds were singing, bees were dancing amongst the flowers. And it was dancing, I was completely certain. The news that somewhere, on the other side of my host nation, two million people had been vaporized or incinerated—or worse, had been afflicted with radiation poisoning and would now die slow, painful deaths—was an abstract construct I couldn't wrap my mind around no matter how hard I tried.

After lunch, an elder beckoned me into the auditorium once more.

"Well?" she asked, once we passed beyond the doors and speech was allowed. Many other initiates stood along the walls of the room, each in hushed conversation with an elder. This was apparently as much privacy as the situation would allow.

My mind churned for some time. I think I stood with my mouth agape. All I could think about was how I had passed green after the second attempt and red, orange and yellow at only one attempt each. My whole life had built up to this point. I had studied so hard, learned a difficult foreign tongue, cast away all my worldly positions, relocated myself across three thousand miles of ocean, and yet now, of all times, my world had the gall to go to war.

A part of me told myself that I should worry about my parents, my brother, and my friends from college, but they hardly seemed real anymore.

My upcoming attempt at blue felt real.

Was any of this normal? Was this unnatural? Had my single-minded desire turned me into a callous monster? Was this some reaction to fear? Perhaps I was trying to find any means necessary of staying cloistered within the Order's secure walls. Even the most aggressive countries don't drop bombs on tiny islands populated only by religious orders.

"I'll stay," I whispered.

The elder nodded and led me out of the auditorium.

Three days later, I failed to reach blue.

That moment marked the low point of my entire time at the Temple of Setting Sun, although, to be fair, it was also the most socially awkward. In the days after the declaration of war and the initial drop of bombs upon numerous countries across the world, a kind of muted, awkward hatred began to stir amongst the initiates and elders of the Order.

I found my own feelings confused. I'd tried not to look too hard while reading the sheet of paper that contained the list of which countries were at war with which. I'd just wanted to spot my own. And certainly the list had not been distributed or made available to any initiates since. However, I had spotted a few country names, and the physical features of people from those countries were very prominent, and, being human, I could not help but feel a... a something awful welling up within me when I met an initiate or elder of such a nationality.

I recognized this as racism right away, and my conscious mind told me I should not be judging a member of the human species for crimes his tribesmen may or may not have committed.

And yet the feeling remained.

I persisted for only a few days more. Numerous initiates and elders vanished abruptly—there at breakfast, and suddenly absent from the twilight ceremony. We couldn't talk within the temple, of course, but we didn't have to. It was obvious. They'd decided to return to whatever country they called home, or what was left of it. It was worst during the first week, then tapered off to a trickle, just one or two a day after that.

Today, I would say that roughly half the original population of the Order remains from what it was two weeks prior.

Without a single bomb, we too have been halved.

The muted conversation still rumbles behind me, the violation of our Ultimate Protocol, committed by the very elders who must enforce the holy silence within our walls.

Still engulfed in the surreal calm of the chirping and the breeze and the buzzes of insects, I stand and walk away from this part of the garden and the blasphemous door behind it.

I make my way down the eastern path, along the stream, past another hill. A dozen or so initiates sit in meditation, circled around the trunk of a tall pine. I pass them and hurry to the door that leads to the auditorium. I do not enter, but instead gaze at the computer panel at the door.

It registers the presence of radiation within the atmosphere, but the levels have remained relatively low. The knowledge that somewhere, hundreds or thousands of kilometers away, people are dying in the thousands or millions, that they could be my countrymen, skids across my consciousness leaving dark streaks. I close my eyes and take a deep breath. I push the thoughts away.

I remind myself that purple is only nine days away. In nine days, I will attempt purple. And with the last color, there is no color. If the initiate makes purple, he or she pushes immediately past to whatever lies beyond, that secret which only elders of the Order know, and of which none speak, because to speak is to taint thought, to make it into something constructed, transmitted, and inevitably miscomprehended.

But to think, now, some new event, some horror or atrocity, has driven an *elder* to speak within the purely silent temple interior... If not radiation, if not another bomb, what could it be? Will we be called into the auditorium again, I wonder?

That moment never comes.

I try to find the quietest corner of the expansive gardens that I can, which is easy now that we number so few, and I sit and I stare. My new vantage point presents me with a hazy view of the western mountain range. Its tops are capped with snow and I watch a mist roll in off the ocean, which ducks in to the valley north of us, just between us and the mountains. The beach is about a half day's walk from here.

Some initiates have trouble with the elevation. It's never bothered me.

I sit through the afternoon, focusing my breathing and my mind. My stomach grumbles audibly on numerous occasions, but I decide to skip dinner all the same. The sun grows lower and lower in the sky, which turns a dull shade of red. A squawking flock of birds, which only comes out in the evening, begin their twilight reverie, signaling to initiates and elders alike that our rite atop the hills is upon us.

I walk down from my vantage point into the garden proper, and make my way to my usual hill. I join my peers, the four of them that remain, and the two elders assigned to us atop our designated hill. I am the last to arrive.

The stares of my colleagues are blank and empty. The news of the war has left those of us who remain with little to express upon our faces or with our gestures. I wonder if they feel as hollow as me inside, but there's no way to find out. Upon this hill, one of us is undoubtedly at war with another, but if we care, I can't tell. At least, we know we are not supposed to, and the animosity I noticed in the first few days has waned. And yet, twenty, thirty, forty years of societal conditioning and allegiance and family and friends cannot be wiped out by all this serenity.

Do they feel something underneath their empty facades? Do they struggle, like me, to contain the anger and the pain, and the worry, and the heartbreak—the thought of my baby brother picking up a weapon, or pushing a button that will drop a bomb. He likes computers—is he programming the targeting system for something that will kill? Will my blood spill the blood thousands of others, if only indirectly? Am I culpable for the actions of my nation state? Did they drop the bombs on this one?

Our faces are blank and empty.

We sit, and we raise our palms toward the mountains and the setting sun. We let out a dull, long hum, the letter "m," not words or speech, the only vocalization allowed within our walls.

I push my pain out with the sound, and hope that by evacuating it, I will be able to pass beyond purple and end this bizarrely torturous waking dream.

Three days pass normally after hearing the elder's outburst in the garden. I do not know the elder who spoke. I have seen him around, but I have never been led by him. I occasionally wonder if he noticed me on that day, but mostly I am able to slip back into my normal routine.

During lunch on the third day, he sits next to me. We're all in the common plaza. I've got my tray with my rice balls and stewed chicken and tea. A pair of bluebirds chirps in the branches of trees, which cover the entire plaza.

And then there he is. He's a tall, lanky elder with a gray beard, and he plops himself down right next to me. His arrival cuts through my concentration over food, but I don't dare look up at him. My spoon wobbles slightly, and a few drops fall off. I manage to recover and bring it to my mouth. I can't remember my last meal that was this uncomfortable.

What does he want? Is this some kind of veiled threat that I not report his outburst?

That evening, after the ceremony, I lie atop my hard mattress with a lump in my throat trying to find myself within my thoughts. I have less than a week until the prismaticum. Part of me feels that if I can make it there, if I can achieve my life's goal, then everything will go back to the way it was before I came here. The war will vanish. I will leave the temple, ride back to the island's capital on a train, then I'll endure the ten hour plane flight home, and everything will be just as it was.

Except I will be different.

I will remember this insanity, this dream of dreams turned to silent nightmare. And I will have to square that with who and what I am.

I know the war will not go away just because I want it to. That's wishful thinking at its most naive.

—

The elder who spoke near me in the garden and who sat near me once at dinner does not come near me again. The night before my prismaticum I hear scuffling feet in the hallway outside my quarters. It sounds like a lot of people and is loud enough to at least partially wake me.

I don't remember it very well the next morning. It feels like the night itself could have been a prismaticum. Perhaps my mind moved me through red, orange, yellow, green, blue and purple to hurried, scuffling footsteps in the need. Perhaps that is my only reward for my endeavors.

I sit up in my bed and lean over, my arms wrapped around my chest, and I weep, wordlessly. They cannot kick me out over sobbing, only words, and I have no words to describe my current predicament, this living simultaneously in wonder and terror.

It is the day of the prismaticum, and so I must eat neither breakfast nor lunch. I will be allowed a second portion at dinner. I spend the day in my secluded area in the back of garden where the ground rises up, and the valley and coast are visible below. I sit and watch all the insects, especially the bees. They always seem to know exactly what they are doing—their dance is flawlessly theirs. They have no existential crises. Any one of them will gladly give their lives for their clan. Not like me, who can't even be bothered to check on my family and friends.

I have left them with only silence.

I worry about them, deep down, and wonder if they are worrying about me. I wonder if they are alive, and I know that I cannot worry this worry right now.

My prismaticum awaits.

I wish I could be more like the bee.

The elder with the gray beard, the one whose speech violated the Ultimate Protocol, he is one of the four who leads my prismaticum today.

We traverse the caverns in absolute silence. The echoes of our footfalls, ten feet all traipsing along uneven rock in a hollow cavern, blend with the dripping water.

Prior journeys here have intensified the serenity that follows morning fast and mediation, even last time when I made it to blue I remember feeling supremely calm. The experience blended into the trance that was the prismaticum. This journey feels different. I am calm, collected, in control, sure. I can feel my whole body, all its movements precisely synced, my mind aware of itself and in control of all its functions.

And I can't help but wonder if this is really good for me? All these practices, all this structure, this ritual, are designed to help me learn more about myself, about the world I live in. I chose the Order of the Setting Sun because it resonated with me on a profound level I can't describe in words, and yet in pursuing this, I have somehow managed to estrange myself from everything in my old life, and in a way that I would not have been comfortable with if I had known this would happen at the start of my journey.

The tunnel opens up into the oval cavern. Water runs in rivulets down the wall, their courses changing from moment to moment, converging and diverging endlessly. I stop and press a finger to the wall. I swipe across, momentarily diverting all the water flows in its path.

The elders stare at me, the one who spoke most piercingly of all.

I walk to the center of the chamber, I sit, and I close my eyes.

I do not reach purple.

This is not at all a surprise.

I struggle even with blue, though I do reach it, eventually. But the whole spectrum collapses shortly thereafter, and the elders lead me out of the oval chamber, through the tunnels and back to the surface.

The moment we exit into the garden, the elder with the beard beckons me. I look him over, and wonder what nationality he is. He does not look like the people of the country we currently inhabit. His skin is the same tone as mine. I wonder if perhaps we share a nationality.

He leads me, as I suspect, to the auditorium. The hallways are dark and empty, and I admit to a certain amount of fear. Members of the Order would never harm another, would they? I have never heard of such a thing, but religious sects have their fair share of scandals. I'm sure mine is no exception.

The auditorium is completely empty, but the elder turns on the lights. He turns to me, his eyes sharp and harsh. "How badly do you want to continue here?"

I am unsure how to answer his question. I feel my heart rate tick up a few notches, and I jam my hands behind my back. "This is all I've ever wanted."

"I am in a very uncomfortable position. I can tell you

something, but—"

His voice continues on, he is saying something about how I might desire to continue, and this would relieve him of his burden if he could hear me say so, but it is too late. He need not go any further. The damage is done. I know it in my gut. I have suspected it for days, pushed it down, hidden it away, pushed it down and down, just like we push the sun down with our collective will in the evening.

"Is it my brother?" I ask.

The color drains out of his face. "Who told you?"

Tears stream down my face. I cannot stop them. "You did. Just now."

"Oh my..."

He embraces me and I sob into his robe.

"My parents?" I am howling.

"They were in the countryside. They're safe... for now, and trying to contact you."

That evening was the last evening I performed the twilight ceremony. The elder with the gray beard walked up the hill behind me. He approached one of the elders who normally led my hill, put a hand on his shoulder and nodded to him. That elder nodded back, then left, descending back down the hill and away.

The birds still sang their evening song and the bees still danced and leaves still drifted silently down onto manicured pools of tiny stones—not a single, meagerest sign of war. No monitor reported dangerously high radiation in the atmosphere, no klaxons sounded the imminent threat of bombs, no notices mentioned suspicious activity amongst governmental reports. The

Temple of the Setting Sun is a small compound with limited technology situated on a strategically uninteresting island many miles off the coast of its host country's mainland.

And yet, as I sat atop that hill, and pushed the sun downward with my hands, for the first time, I felt as though its dim light and heat were searing into me, flaying me alive. I wondered what my brother had felt as a nuclear device blew itself, and him, into sub-atomic particles a mile or so above his head.

As soon as the last glimmers of light disappeared behind the mountains, I retracted my hands sharply and rubbed them over one another.

The other initiates and elders stood and turned to move down the hill.

I took a deep breath as they walked away, and I shouted at the top of my lungs to the dead and empty glimmer of light radiating out from behind the rocky spires beyond the temple walls.

Lunar Eclipse

Eslyum 17, Year of His Holiness 763
The journey home felt longer than it ever has before. My hands are still shaking as I write this. Never before have I been more afraid to walk the streets of my home city. But His Holiness has always remained a staunch supporter of the observation of the stars, & I doubt even the events of the past few days could undermine the foundation he provides for our researches. If anything, I have heard that it has only availed Him of its importance.

But politics is not my forte. I shall leave such endeavors in the hands of others, such as Methis. He enjoys hosting guests from the Court.

I sit now in my studio. It is quiet outside, though not the natural quiet of night. I saw fires still burning on my way here and heard shouting in the distance. It was as though I had been transported to another world. But here in Arno district, at least, people have shuttered themselves inside, & the insanity remains at a distance.

It almost makes me wish I had never reported the anomaly. Seven days ago, I spotted it during a routine observation of Luna. A dot in the sky nearby, too big to be a star and also brand new. I estimated it at roughly one twentieth of Luna's size. I wrote up a report immediately, of course, & sent it off to the Court the next morning. I didn't give it much more thought. Shooting stars appear with some frequency, & stars have been known to flare or blink out on occasion. There are even the odd ones whose light waxes and wanes at steady intervals like lighthouse beams. Why not should a new light join Luna, albeit a strange one?

And besides, to the naked eye, it merely looked like a new star.

When I arrived at the observatory the next evening, I observed it again, & was both surprised and alarmed to discover it had grown larger. It had also drawn closer to Luna. Observing with the telescope, it now appeared as an unnaturally large star. I sent for a carriage, went to court, & spoke directly with the Science Minister. I related my findings with some urgency, and he insisted I was overreacting. At the time, I remember feeling somewhat silly, as though I were an unruly child, obstinately demanding attention from parents with better things to do. I went back to the observatory and tried to get on with my evening as best I could.

Oh, how I wish the Minister's judgment had proved correct. By the next evening, our new "star" had grown yet again & drawn even closer to Luna. It could no longer be mistaken for a star. I filed an urgent report and set a courier out with it, not daring to make the journey to Court myself.

That next evening was my last journey from home to the observatory for many evenings. I remember the streets being eerily silent in the twilight, & as I looked up at the sky, I noticed that Luna's new companion was now visible to the naked eye. I hurried onward, rushed into the observatory, and found only a few lab boys present. I asked one of them where everyone was, & he said that the day staff had been summoned to Court. The object had been visible to the city's entire populace since the afternoon.

I took measurements of Luna's Companion in the telescope—who now measured one fourteenth her diameter and four ninths of a tessic to her left—and hurried away to Court. I arrived in the middle of a briefing led by none other than His Holiness and all of His ministers.

Word had arrived that two neighboring nations were in turmoil, & another, it was worried, would use Luna's Companion, dubbed by some imaginative individuals, "Satan's Omen," as an excuse to invade. All maladies of our modern age were being blamed upon this new light in the sky, & some new ones had even been invented, apparently to give Luna's Companion added *raison d'être*. The Court remained concerned about fortifying our borders and keeping order within the city. His Holiness showed calm erudition, as I have come to expect from him.

I returned to the observatory exhausted & with only

a few hours until sunrise. I decided to take one more measurement of Luna's Companion before returning home, and discovered he had grown to one-twelfth Luna's size & had drawn another ninth of a tessic closer.

I gathered up my research notes, ran out of the observatory in the morning light, hurried down the hillside, only to stop dead in my tracks as I gazed out over Prax. Fires had lit up in two districts, smoke bathed the city, & shouting sounded distantly. I hurried to the guards at the observatory gates, who insisted there was nothing to worry about here at the observatory, at least not yet, & I hurried back up to the hill.

I did not sleep during that terrible day.

I alternated between charting the progress of Luna's Companion, & walking out onto the balcony to observe the steady descent of Prax into chaos. Thankfully, the palace, the observatory, the other research labs, and the Tollmy District remained peaceful, albeit unnaturally quiet. As I grew more tired and weary, I could not help but feel I had fallen into some kind of dream world. I suspected I were living in a hallucination of my city, instead of reality. All this insanity over a new light in the sky, albeit the strangest light we had ever seen. & we had thought the uproar during a blood moon was something to remark upon.

Prax burned, & I took all the notes I could. Luna's Companion grew to one-eighth of Luna's diameter, visible to the naked eye in broad daylight, before disappearing behind her completely.

& then nothing. He was gone.

The Militia restored order, slowly throughout the night. I slept during the dark hours for the first time in months, & when I woke the next morning, one of the lab boys was shaking my shoulder with a summons from His Holiness. I reported all my findings, & handed over copies of all my observations.

Luna's Companion was certainly not a star, for it grew too quickly. I suspect it was made of rock or perhaps metal, much as we expect Luna to be. The fact that it has never returned to our view, however, suggests only one thing, I fear. Luna's Companion may have collided with her, albeit on her far side where we would be unable to witness it. & as Luna is locked with her same face always toward us, I fear we may never be able to prove one way or the other exactly what transpired.

I wonder if, perhaps one day, men of Prax may discover a way to fly a man to Luna and verify my hypotheses, but alas, such an observation is beyond the techniques of my age or any I can imagine in the foreseeable future. For now, I shall thank His Holiness for keeping me safe & secure within Prax, & for continuing his most beneficent funding of our studies.

Journal of Chief Researcher Alyias Tiffenmoor III
City of Prax of the Kingdom of Reyyan

———

Eslyum 4, Year of His Holiness 828
I fear for the future of the Shipwright's Guild.

I never thought I would write those words. I am not, in fact, a man of very good words. However, I feel it is important to set down a record of these occurrences. I had heard rumors that the other coastal nations have experienced similar turmoil from their leadership, and even distant landlocked Uyssy has been affected, owing to its heavy reliance on river trade.

Last year, the engineers completed improvements to our docks. They raised the walkways by twenty-four tessics and extended them outward by ten iyals. But the scientists came a week ago and did their measurements during high tide and low tide, and they tell me that high tide is up one-seventh of a tessic over last year, and low tide is down by the same amount. Four years ago, when we asked for these improvements, the tides were only changing by one-fourteenth of a tessic, and the scientists had speculated this to a temporary climatic shift that would eventually equalize out across the globe. They now mumble about a problem that will grow worse with time.

And that leaves me in the unfortunate position of having signed the requisition on expensive improvements, which we thought would keep sea trade going indefinitely. It now appears as though, even if the current rate of tidal modulation holds steady, these the docks will need to be raised and extended again in just over a decade.

There is also the matter of what seamen are reporting these days. Some of their sturdiest regiments have complained of enormous swells causing terrible seasickness during storms. Our best ships return from routine trade routes battered, vastly depleting the profit of oceanic trade.

I will keep the guild going as best I'm able, but I fear that I will not remain in the Court's favor much longer. I fear also for the scientists. As the economy grows unstable, their funding will dry up as well. Only the Militia will remain.

I am no longer certain of the future as I once was, since I now believe sea trade is on a trajectory to end forever. But for now, the Glorious State of Reyyan has trade relationships to maintain, and I will serve His Holiness to the best of my abilities until the end of my days.

Sergeant Captain Oysolus Pyintooth
Head of the Oceanic Trade Guild of the City of Prax,
Kingdom of Reyyan

—

Guard this book with your life.

Those in power do not wish to accept the truth, but here it is. Even in an era when the odds of surviving sea travel are on par with the flip of the coin, we, the proudest and noblest of the citizens of Prax, have found it necessary to risk death, both from the wild seas and from our own compatriots, to travel to distant lands and form a fairer union, one not based on heredity or blind faith, but on the science that can save us from the calamities of the modern age.

We do not blame the king and his staff for wanting to protect what they have, but we do blame them for not being reactive to the needs of their subjects. As tides erode the coasts of our cities by tessics a year, and ever faster, how long will it be before Prax and its neighbors are swallowed up entirely?

The citizens of New Prax shall form land and water pacts that will ensure our survival and not allow our new country to get crushed into another inland empire.

It is unlikely, as the oceans grow more and more turbulent, that we will be able to maintain contact with our homeland for more than a couple of decades, but we wish for them to know that we did not abandon them in spirit or in faith, merely wished to be free to diverge from them in matters of social and economic organization. All nations must adapt to the reality of our world's increasing tidal instability. Any nation that does not risks being destroyed by it.

Arkys Kly, author of *Social Reformation for Stability in an Unstable World*
Kly Settlement, Capitol of the Republic of New Prax
Eslyum 18, y. 871

———

Eslyum 9, y. 939
I fear that Brayen and I will never speak again.

For men who have saved each other's lives time and time again, the situation is surreal. He saved me from plummeting off Mount Iiyis, and yet we have no words for one another.

He still insists there is, in fact, no hope. I argue *Social Reformation*'s points, and he is deaf to them. Perhaps, if I walk through his views once more, here on paper, I will finally see in them what he does, for I wish to bridge this gap.

As we have heard from the Old World, the countries of our ancestors have fallen into war, famine, and internecine strife. Sea trade, while still barely possible along the coasts, is no longer profitable, and zones of arable farmland change year over year. Whereas we in New Prax have flexible borders and have established strict ecological zoning rules for new settlements, the citizens of the old countries find their coastal borders eroding year over year and political pressure from their inland neighbors to make military funding an ever-increasing priority.

We have no inland neighbors, and their establishment is forbidden.

And yet, Brayen sees a time in our future when the tides will rise up to lick the bases of mountains, like the many ranges we passed over together in our survey of these new lands.

I know that the tides increase now by whole tessics a year, and there is really no reason to see them slowing down, but really? Tides miles high that will sweep away everything from our modern coasts through hundreds of ebjas of prairies and marshes and flatlands?

Brayen admits that *Social Reformation* is an improvement upon the Old World, but he does not believe our way of life here will suffice us forever. He talks about the scientists at New Prax Observatory having made a discovery that the moon is growing closer to the earth, and linking its decaying orbit to the tidal changes. It will grow closer and closer and then smash into us, he says. Our expedition was for naught. *Social Reformation* is for naught, he said, while drunk. I had to take him out of the bar, for ruffians nearly started a fight with him over his "unpatriotism." If they knew who he was, they would eat those words.

Whenever anyone looks upon a map of this continent

for the next thousand years, whenever anyone wishes to plan their county's borders against tidal change, they need thank Brayen. He and I spent our lifetimes charting this continent, its rivers, and its lakes. Brayen was the cartographer, I the survivalist. We saved each other's lives millions of times over.

And he insists it was all for naught.

Those in the old country are fond of thinking that no matter what calamity befalls them, their king will find a way. Like most of this country, I don't have much fondness for kings. I believe that science will find a way. Brayen does not, but I love him regardless, and I still would not think twice to trade my life for his.

Eklo Mulni, a letter to a friend,
included in the second edition of
Brayen and Eklo's Charts of the Continental Interior

—

A Theory of Tidal Forces on Solar Bodies
Myri Klaiss
University of New Prax
Geological and Astrophysical Sciences Department
Published Eslyum 20, y. 1001

ABSTRACT: There exists a relationship between any two solar bodies in which one is orbiting the other, such that each body exerts a gravitational force on the other. In addition, there exists a physical limit, roughly equal to two and a half radii of the larger body, whereby the smaller body, should it fall within this limit, shall be subjected to tidal forces strong enough to tear it apart.

This theory accounts for the existence of rings around the larger planets of Meyr and Limmlys. It posits that the rings are in fact the fragmented rocks of lunar bodies which fell inside Meyr and Limmlys's respective physical limits. The distance of Meyr and Limmlys's extant moons from their respective surfaces is consistent with this theory (they remain intact because they occupy stable orbits outside of the limit).

In contrast to the *Theory of the Millennial Calamity* of Rey, Klynn, Trubas, and Nyrman (y. 992, University of Tybyng), which describes the tidal forces of the moon's decaying orbit causing increasing geological disturbances and tidal differentials until the moon's eventual impact with the earth in y. 2015, the proposed theory of tidal forces and solar bodies posits that, instead, the moon will fall inside the earth's tidal limit zone in y. 1483, and at that point will be fragmented into a disc of particulate rock similar to the rings of Meyr of Limmlys.

—

We find ourselves now at the median moment. It is roughly three hundred years since Tiffenmoor recorded his observations of the Lunatic Object, and four hundred years until the dissolution of the moon into particulate ring matter once it falls inside the Klaiss Limit, the theory now widely believed to be the most accurate prediction as to the fate of our planetary ecosystem.

And here we are, about to launch an expedition back

to the Old World, a place sealed off to us for over century due to tidal fluctuations so great that ocean travel is no longer possible. At the present moment, the Grennat Ocean, when our moon is behind us is reduced to three-quarters of its depth when our moon lies directly above us.

The stories our ancestors tell us of times when the tidal differential was measured in tessics seem like stories from scientific romance periodicals. And yet, this is our world's history.

Arkys Kly and the original settlers of New Prax had much to begrudge the monarchy they left behind. But just because we could not agree on how best to govern ourselves does not mean that we wish to forsake them to the ravages of a changing world. Our cultural heritage was birthed from theirs. Their blood is our blood. And we all know the saying about blood and water. Rising tides have no business keeping us apart.

As we usher in the age of aeronautics and rediscover the land we lost contact with, the land that made our ancestors who they were, and made us who we are today, let us remember that although our ancestors left Prax on less than friendly terms, we have every reason in the present to renew our common bond of humanity with our forbearers.

I wish the First Aeronautical Exploratory Team of New Prax success in their expedition to the Old World. Good luck and good fortune.

President Ely Goldmyn
from a speech given at Kly International Airfield
Eslyum 1, 1084 CE

Alli Nymitt
4480 Harywy Street #202
Oceana City, Republic of New Prax 99B-C72
Eslyum 5, 1149 CE

Dear Markys,

How I wish you were here, my dear! It feels odd at times, looking up and seeing the plexiglass overhead, the sky warped and skewed behind it. And it really is foreboding, the first time you hear the tidal bulge rolling in and the crashing overhead. I was in a restaurant, and I flinched and cowered a bit, and everyone else just went on eating. The second time it happened, I was outdoors, and I was able to watch as it rolled over the dome and blotted out the sky.

The city is bright, with lots of signs and street lamps, and the streets are always clean. The city is awash with energy, as they have so much room on either side to put out tidal generators. They say that Oceana sits on the land that was the first Kly International Airport, the place where President Goldmyn gave his famous address. Hard to believe. You look outside the dome and it's just barren.

I read in a research paper the other day about a historian who thinks that if we didn't have all this tidal and geothermal energy available we would have gone on burning oil. Hard to believe. Can you imagine the energy expenditure digging it all up? Doesn't seem worth it. But you're the geophysicist. Does that sound plausible to you?

Everyone at the office is friendly. I'm really digging this new job, too. But I miss you desperately. I can't wait for you to join me in Oceana. Tell me again when you'll make it here. I know it's only two months away, but I wish it were now. I can't wait to show you the sights.

Yours,
Alli

—

And so, we hope that it is now clear from the given evidence that the climate of our planet is indeed undergoing a warming transformation. While naysayers still remain in every country on earth, there is overwhelming evidence from all areas of the geophysical and climatological scientific communities that the earth is indeed warming, and that the gravitational stress of the moon upon the earth is indeed the culprit.

We have clear records of increased vulcanism going back over two centuries, and climatological data for an even longer period.

It is the recommendation of this panel that the nations of the earth come to an agreement to form an international scientific body dedicated to the exploration of solutions that will keep the earth's biosphere intact in the remaining two hundred and eighty years before the moon will be torn apart when it falls inside the Klaiss Limit.

from a report submitted to the International Panel
on Climate Change and Geological Instability
Eslyum 22, 1207 CE

—

ALYX: Next you'll be telling me that the moon isn't round anymore.

METT: ...

ALYX: The moon isn't round, is it?

METT: It's mostly round.

ALYX: Mostly doesn't count!

METT: Do you want to know what it looks like?

ALYX: I guess.

METT: It's a lot larger than that, for one. *points at the sky*. And it's kind of ovular. Like an orange that's been squished a little.

ALYX: *laughs*

METT: What?

ALYX: You said 'ovular.'

METT: So what?

ALYX: The doesn't mean 'shaped like an oval.' It means 'having to do with ovaries.'

METT: *rolls eyes* Whatever.

ALYX: *grins* Come here.

METT: *draws closer* What?

ALYX: I don't care what the moon's shaped like in the future. Or even if the whole world falls apart. I just want to be with you for whatever time we've got.

from *Alyx and Mett* season 1 episode 14, an award-winning serial television drama about a couple in which one partner, Mett, is a fourteenth-century climate refugee who travels back in time to the tenth century; first aired Eslyum 7, 1272 CE

—

Although the geological stress, which in turn causes vulcanism and atmospheric heating, is the most widely discussed issue of the day, I respectfully submit to the Consortium that our most pressing concerns are yet to come.

First, the problem of the tidal bulge obliterating huge tracts of forests is well known. The relationship that boreal organisms possess to climate regulation is well documented. However, the discovery of forms of phytoplankton within the tidal bulge, particular Mikosia Phelotypa, as documented by Captain Remaar of the Tideship Endeavor, gives reason for hope that the biology of this planet will adapt to the changing conditions.

Even if the worst estimates prove true, global temperatures will only increase by an average of five degrees by 1483, the year of Klaiss's prediction of the moon's destruction. Five degrees is a significant change, but it is one that we have reason to believe that we and the biosphere can outlive, especially since the increased vulcanism would end once the moon has broken up.

What should be worrisome to everyone is what energy sources we will use to power humanity's massive technological infrastructure after the moon's dissolution. We currently operate on an enormous surplus of power, generated primarily from tidal turbines as the tidal bulge traverses our planet one and a half times daily, and whose speed and intensity only grow stronger as time progresses. That tidal bulge will cease the moment our moon fragments, as will any and all tidal activity whatsoever.

And if we are worried about climate change now, we should be worried about what climate change will look like in the next century. With no external gravitational force (save for the weak force exerted by the sun), the stirring effect in the oceans will be greatly reduced, with only a small amount occurring around our planet's equator.

In addition, our moon currently acts a stabilizing force against wobbling in our planet's tilt. At this stage, we can only speculate what such a change would mean for our planet's climate systems.

It is the recommendation of this researcher that we refocus our efforts from mitigating warming to preparing ourselves for the terrific climate changes that will occur when our moon falls inside the Klaiss Limit in one hundred and thirty years.

from a recommendation submitted to the World Consortium on Mitigating Climate Change and Geological Instability by Dr. Julyanna Halgyr on Eslyum 11, 1348 CE

—

I looked out the window, and it was so close. This rocky landscape that we've all seen above our heads, all cracked and bloated, and even though it looked like this big gray eggshell that someone had begun to smash at, I could see, through all the fractures and slabs, this enormous crater, just huge, covering probably a quarter of the moon's surface. If that meteor didn't hit the equator exactly, it was damn close.

And I remembered something that Tiffenmoor guy wrote, way back, more than seven hundred years ago, about this white dot in the sky that wasn't a star, getting closer and closer to the moon, and then it was just gone, and how he wished he could have seen what had happened, and he hoped that one day some person would.

Well, Dr. Tiffenmoor, here I am, looking down at what would have been the biggest explosion humanity had ever seen, if it hadn't been on the wrong side of the moon. I don't think anyone's going to be landing down there, but boy, this is one hell of a view.

Veyga Irstyng, during an interview he participated
in from the New Prax Spaceship Arkys 4
Eslyum 17, 1410 CE

—

Our beacon fractured
its guiding beam sputters
Meaning suffers, too
What henceforth shall be a 'month'?
Within one generation
a tidal bulge is diminished to a tidal swell
Glimmering fragments spread
from an oblong blister in the sky

outward
Will the rings sparkle, I wonder?
Our tidal cities collapse into disuse
plexiglass falling away
to dry and barren earth
one by one
A brilliance
gone from our sky
Inspiring us throughout the ages
We gave you gods, you know
In some cultures
you were a god yourself
But even gods can suffer mortal wounds
it would seem
We shall see how well humanity fares
without your guiding light

Lunar Eclipse, by Baakyo Melma
from his poetry chapbook of the same title, first
published Eslyum 17, 1471

We Were Here First

Bruce pulled open the door to the public house with a mighty gasp. He glanced about the dimly lit room, clasping his right bicep with his left hand. Some eyes turned toward him, but not many. Good.

He scanned the interior of the pub, quickly assessing the counter on the right and the oaken tables scattered throughout the room. He let his gaze stop only briefly on the buxom barmaid. In other circumstances he might have evaluated how he might best court her, but so many other matters pressed on his mind this evening that his carnal impulses would have to wait. In the back of the large space, he spotted a group of tables half-secluded by a partial wall and window panes—a cloister of sorts. Its tables lay empty.

Bruce hobbled quickly toward it. He hoped his leg

was not bleeding too badly. He'd been to public houses in Reiar that would actually turn away the wounded at the first sign of running blood, even those who bore a royal crest upon their breastplate. A few more eyes strayed his way as he shuffled across the wooden floorboards, but no one moved to stop him. He half-hoped the barmaid would, but she paid him no mind.

He found the table at the farthest back corner of the pub, in a small area of three tables, partitioned off from the main chamber by an additional wall. He threw down his two packs, and slowly lowered himself into the chair. His leg and arm ached, and pain seared within them anew. He took deep breaths as he slowly unwrapped the bandage on his arm, threw it into the pack for dirty things and retrieved a clean one from the pack for clean things. The dirty pack had begun to bulge and his supplies in the clean pack had reached critically low levels. And he still had miles left to travel through Reiar.

His arm seemed fine; he could still move his fingers. That arrow had just glanced his shoulder. His leg, however, was worse. He winced through the pain as he changed its bandage. Eventually, with both wounds staunched, he pulled up a second chair, put up his bad leg and leaned back in his seat. He scanned the pub again briefly—still no sign that anyone cared about his presence—so he closed his eyes and tilted his chair back into the wall.

"Milord?" a voice before him.

His eyes shot open. "Yes?"

A young man stood before him, clearly the youngest of the staff. "What can we do for you this evening, milord? Do you require assistance? A drink? Lodging?"

Annoyance that they'd sent this stupid squire instead of the hot barmaid surged within him anew. "Any news of the road to Yvenia this evening?"

"I have heard nothing out of the ordinary, milord."

"Good. You may go." Bruce closed his eyes and leaned back again.

He would restock in Yvenia. This town, whatever its name was, would not offer him sufficient protection from his pursuers. There were, however, people in Yvenia who owed him a favor or two. If he could just get there he could finally get some sleep.

"Hi!"

The voice sounded female, and Bruce imagined that the buxom barmaid had decided to join him, but when he opened his eyes, he started at the sight of a young man, who stood across the table from him. He had done up his hair, and his clothing bore flamboyant frills. Clearly a poofter. Revulsion surged through Bruce, and the poofter's smile faded.

Three women came in behind him, one middle-aged and the other two the same age as the poofter. The poofter, to Bruce's horror, threw his things down on Bruce's table, right across from him. Just threw them down across from a man bearing the leather armor and royal sigil of Jeia! The two younger and reasonably attractive women joined him at Bruce's table, opening up bags and producing scrolls, parchment, and quills. The older woman seated herself gracefully at an adjacent table.

The women had done up their clothes, too. They wore bulky but very extravagant dresses, but there was something not quite right about the styles, something artificial, something feigned—and that's when it dawned on him—they were performers.

"What is going on?" Bruce asked the group.

"I am Madam Origoire of the Northwest Reiar Theatre Company." No 'milord'. No recognition of his title. Nothing.

"I've had quite an evening," Bruce snarled.

The group of them nodded, and their smiles drooped, but continued pulling out their parchments and quills and setting them on Bruce's table.

Bruce huffed. "Now look here!"

The theatre troupe's movements slowed, and they eyed him warily but made no move to leave their seats.

"I've had a very difficult journey, and I just need a couple hours silence, if that's alright."

"Our troupe has reserved this space," Madam Origoire said. "Every Amnday from midnight 'til dawn."

Bruce furrowed his brow. "Reserved? In a public house?"

"Yes," Madam Origoire responded matter-of-factly.

"How are you feeling? Better?" The poofter asked Madam Origoire.

"Yes!" she replied jovially. "Actually much since last week."

"Splendid," the poofter replied with a disgustingly effeminate wave of his hand. He turned to his colleague at the table beside him. "Those are beautiful quills! Did you get them from Master Trellain's?"

"I did. I noticed them yesterday and just had to pick some up."

"I'll have to get some for myself next week."

Bruce's frustration boiled over. "Do you mind?"

The troupe's expressions soured into frowns once more.

Bruce huffed. "Do you usually... converse at these meetings?"

The poofter snickered, but then silenced himself as Bruce's glare turned toward him.

"Yes, *milord*," the poofter said. "Our performances do require some amount of conversation to work out."

Bruce pushed himself up out of his chair, and hobbled away toward the bar while the troupe snickered behind him. He came to the counter, and clasped the cold metallic edge with both hands.

"Excuse me!" he called to the buxom barmaid, the one who should be servicing him in more ways than one.

She caught his eye, finished pouring a draught, then picked up a rag, cleaned a part of the counter, and finally wended toward him. "Yes, milord?" Her tone was hostile and forced. He'd have to go easy.

"There seems to be some kind of theatre troupe in the back room there—"

"That would be the Northwest Reiar Theatre Troupe, milord."

"Yes. I had set myself up there, but they just barged in and threw down their things—"

"They are very amenable to others using the tables with them, milord."

"Yes, but they are quite... grotesque, if you catch my drift." The barmaid's frown deepened. He'd heard this about Reiar. They were famous for their tolerance of queerdom. "Anyway, it is difficult for me to rest my eyes with them there..." Bruce rolled his hand in the air, hoping the barmaid would catch his drift.

"With them doing what, milord?"

"You know. Talking."

"This is a public house, milord."

"That it is."

"People may talk in a public house, milord, at any table they choose."

"But do they get to use that space exclusively?"

"No, milord. But as I said, they have been very amenable to others using the space with them."

"So, you can't kick them out?"

"I'm afraid not, milord." The barmaid hurried away.

Bruce sighed and begrudgingly hobbled away, back towards the poofter and the crone and the young women who liked the company of poofters better than real men like him. Such an off-kilter country, Reiar. He couldn't wait to get to Yvenia. Best brothels on the whole damn continent. He'd get some nice play there. Presuming his leg healed properly by then.

He threw himself back into his chair, put up his leg, and eyed Madam Origoire. The poofter was saying something to her, but Bruce talked over him. "I talked to the owner of the establishment and she said that you don't get exclusive use of this room or any of the tables."

Madam Origoire turned her gaze slowly toward him. "And neither, milord, do you."

"Yes, but you were wrong." With that, Bruce leaned back and closed his eyes. At least the tones in which the troupe talked were more sedate thereafter. Bruce lost himself in his thoughts. He wondered what the king would have to say about Bruce's report on what had happened to him in Calens. With Reiar in between them and his home country of Jeia, it was unlikely that the two nations would come to blows. But still. If diplomatic relations broke down completely...

A low rumble from somewhere above, at the very periphery of Bruce's perceptions, grew louder, demanded his attention, crescendoing into a roar. Bruce's eyes shot open. The whole public house had grown deathly silent as tables and chairs and beer steins all rattled, patrons and employees both staring up at the ceiling. The noise suddenly ceased, and while most of the staff and patrons remained stunned, a few rushed up out of their seats and out the door.

The troupe stayed put, but Bruce pulled himself up, and hobbled to the door himself. Never had he heard such a cacophony as blared through the sky above him.

He exited and turned, discerning a crowd in the dark night, distinguishable by the light of a few torches held aloft. But that light was nothing compared to the bright white glowing thing that was descending into the forest behind the public house.

"What the devil?" Bruce muttered. People ran about and around him, some carrying weapons, most carrying torches.

The large group down the road began toward the thing in the woods, which had now descended below the tree line, though its bright white light still lit up the sky and made the green of the leaves and underbrush visible despite the night.

Bruce followed, albeit more slowly on his injured leg. He pushed ever forward, stopping to climb over logs and pull himself out of brambles.

He found the group from the village stopped at the edge of a grove, which was brilliantly lit up, as bright as though it were day. The light emanated from an enormous metallic bubble that sat on the ground atop little metallic feet. Fear convected off the herd of villagers in waves, all standing morbidly still. They stared at a trio of strange men, who puttered about near the metal contraption, each wearing the most bizarre clothing and tapping at little rectangular hunks of metal in their hands.

"Hey there!" Bruce shouted.

A small gasp went up from the crowd of villagers. The eyes of the three men turned toward him.

Bruce hobbled into the clearing. "Yes, you! On the authority of the Kingdom of Jeia I demand to know why you have invaded this land, Jeia's friend and ally, the Kingdom of Reiar."

The three men shared bemused glances, then their attention returned to Bruce.

Bruce drew closer to them. "Well?"

"We represent a higher authority," one of the men said.

"Which land do you call home then, that you can craft metallic steeds as bright as the sun that fly through the air?"

The men went back to poking at their metal rectangles.

"Excuse me. You are addressing a knight of the Kingdom of Jeia!"

One of the men shot him a look. "You are excused."

Fear shot through Bruce. What could such people as these do if he angered them? Was their weapons technology on par with their modes of transportation?

"Good sirs," Bruce tried again. "Look at these fine people here. You have most certainly upset them. As a representative of a nearby kingdom, I can use my authority to ease their worry if I can only understand your intentions better—"

"That won't be necessary," one of them men said while his compatriots continued tapping. "They will lose the capacity for abstract reasoning within the next ten minutes, as will you."

"I don't understand—"

"And in under an hour, you will understand even less. We have released a number of genetic modification drones into the environment. Most of you will all be very different creatures within the hour."

Bruce gulped. "What kind of creatures?"

"You have pigs, don't you? Something like that."

Fear shot through Bruce anew, then rage. "Don't do that to us! Please. I beg you. We're not... you can't just..."

"But we can," the man said. "Our ship is badly damaged and in need of repairs. If this planet were protected, that would be one thing, but the Galactic Consortium's designation for your world is Delta-Four. Unprotected and unmanaged. We can make whatever modifications to the environment we please."

"Gal-tic Consortium? What country are they? Where is their stronghold?"

That got the two other men chuckling, as well as Bruce's interlocutor.

"Farther away than your feeble mind can imagine," the man said.

Bruce reached for his knife, pulled it out and

slammed it into his interlocutor's neck. Instead of slicing through his target, Bruce's hand was forced away. He lost his balance and fell into the grass, but caught a glimpse of the man's whole body shimmering.

The crowd at the edge of the forest shouted and dispersed into the trees.

"Even if you were to kill us, it wouldn't stop the drones. You and every person within about a hundred kilometers will change."

"Why?" Bruce gasped.

"As I explained, our ship is damaged," the man said. "Our crew is hungry, and also rather tense, if you catch my drift. They need some appropriate companions for relaxation and recreation. Oh, don't look at me like that. Not all of you will be turned into pigs. Some of you will just get fitter and leaner, better... endowed. But even in such cases, the mind has to go."

"Savages!" Bruce shouted.

They laughed at him. All three of them laughed.

"This is our land!"

Their laughter intensified.

"We were here first!" Bruce tried.

The man shrugged. "We were here second."

Bruce scrambled to a stance and ran. Perhaps he could outrun this change. Perhaps he could stay himself.

He ran to the public house and threw open the door. The whole room was now eerily desolate. He grabbed up his two packs, then hobbled out and down the road as fast as he could away from the horrible light still shining up out of the woods. He kept on furiously thinking as he ran into the night, without a torch, down a road only dimly lit by the moon. He felt as though, if he kept on thinking, he could keep thoughts in his head, that they wouldn't flitter away from him, like the strange men had said they would. He had lost his knife, he realized. No defense from brigands, but that was of negligible concern now—he directed all his effort into escaping those strange men in that terrible grove and thinking, desperately thinking.

Perhaps it had been a dream. Perhaps any moment he would awaken, sitting tilted back in his chair in the public house. He would give anything for the company of Madam Origoire, the poofter, and those two women right now. And he'd stop calling men like the young performer poofters, he decided. He might even go to a few shows in Jeia the next time he had the opportunity.

A pain flared through his back and he fell to the dark ground. The two packs fell off his back and rolled away. He gasped and gasped. The pain in his leg and arm grew more intense, then he realized it was in both legs and both arms. His whole body spasmed, and he yelled. The sound of his voice changed.

Thought drifted away. He stomped his hooves and sniffed with his snout. An irresistible desire for eating truffles and rolling in mud overwhelmed his thoughts. He meandered off the dirt path, and into the underbrush of the forest, looking for both.

AESTHETIC

The second major theme I see evolving in my writing from 2017 forward is the subject of aesthetics, and I believe it is closely intertwined with society.

The formal definition of "aesthetic" is that which concerns itself with the appreciation of beauty. More broadly speaking, aesthetic refers to sets of principles underlying artistic movements, or even unique to particular artists.

Another ramification of the neoliberalism I spoke of in the last section preface is the destruction of aesthetic in the second sense. Increasingly over my lifetime, perhaps even for decades before that, individuals have been taught more and more to fall back on their own determinations of value in order to arbitrate good and bad. Aesthetic judgments have become increasingly reduced to personal preference, and personal preference has become increasingly immune to alteration at another's behest.

This is a case of "solving a problem too far." I am very familiar with the difficulty science fiction has had in climbing out of the literary ghetto imposed by an elite, who insisted quite wrongly for decades that realism and only realism was the true and valid genre aesthetic of literature. Such entrenched power requires us to have the ability to question the norms imposed by those in power.

But our opposition has advanced much too far. We now live in a world where the trashy and the mundane pose as legitimate science fiction art, where we speak of "the golden age of television" as the pinnacle of modern storytelling, where the speculative fiction writers granted cultural access are overwhelmingly derisive of literature and aesthetics as a whole. They speak about monetizing their work on digital retailers instead of how to use the genre as a channel for cognition and perception of the human condition. This is the mob rule version of the appreciation of beauty; it has come around full circle so that hideousness, rather than beauty, is the object of attention. Most can't tell it's a sham. We have allowed so much individual taste to dominate cultural mindspace, and made individuals so resistant to having their enjoyments questioned, that poor taste has been legitimated by virtue of being allowed to snowball into "cultural phenomena."

The only thing a reasonably intelligent, sensitive, well-read individual can do is opt out of this entire system, approaching the artifacts of modern culture with extreme skepticism.

The short stories in this section come at this issue from two different angles. In *Right and Proper*, the setting of the action is an energy production facility that generates its power by obliterating beauty from parallel universes. In *Conifer*, the aesthete protagonist finds his appreciative model thwarted by an art piece that is not what it seems. The conflict serves as a not-so-subtle reminder that while art nourishes the soul, our bodies need nourishment, too. We cannot have the former without the maintenance of the latter.

Although I cannot abide by the aesthetic of my modern day, I can reach into the past, to Shelley, Verne, and Wells, to Le Guin and Ballard, and even, I look with some small amount of hope, to Miéville as a writer in our time producing a legitimate science fictional aesthetic.

The prevailing social order will not last much longer anyhow. The strain on our environment, and even the growing tension within society itself is readily evident. On the other side, I hope, is a real science fiction aesthetic waiting to be born, perhaps even something post-science-fictional. Until then, I present my meager offerings to my readers, and to the world yet to be, beyond me and my time.

Conifer

"It's a bit..." I struggle for the right word. "Solemn. A bit too dreary." I roll my hand in the air. "I mean, yes, it's definitely an immaculate construction. The attention to detail is apparent. But the angles are a little too similar, the needles a bit too smooth. It's a bit too..."

"Piney?" Steward's boy suggests.

I manage to conceal a wince at the youth's inarticulate neologism. "Something like that, yes."

Steward herself frowns. "I think the skill behind this one is rather adept."

I smile gently and raise my hand, hoping to find the skill that Steward has perceived from its tactile properties, if nothing else. I brush my fingers over the needles and this time my disdain slips out. I frown. "And see. The rigidity is all just... And it's all the same shade of blue! Not a single gradient to be found."

The tree looms, casting a divisive shadow between me and Steward. The boy looks up at me with twisted lips. Last year the boy had asked me why I never like the 'cool' trees. His mother, distressed, apologized for his outburst, but I smiled and calmly explained to the boy that some adults find more fault in things than children do because they have learned to appreciate the finer points of aesthetics better than children. Children may find an old thing of any ridiculous quality amusing. Aesthetes, like myself, have developed the sense to appreciate that which is truly beautiful.

At that point, I believe I emphasized my words with a flourish of my hands. At which point I realized the boy had fixed his attention on another tree. And Steward began scolding him before I could say anything more.

He is Steward's son, so he'll doubtless gain some appreciation of the sublime. Eventually.

We walk to the next tree, this one tall and very green. The green has almost a neon glow. Very garish. And I find the angles jarring. Even Steward is wincing at this one. But the boy loves it. He's already pressing his fingertips into the needles.

"Charlie!" Steward says. "What did I tell you about that?"

"Sorry, mom." The boy is not sorry.

Steward turns to me. "N?"

"N," I confirm. The lowest evaluation.

We move on to the next. The boy's eyes go wide, and he turns up his nose. We all sniff the air. This tree exudes a scent most peculiar. It tickles the nose, suffuses the throat.

My eyes scan it. It is quite the conundrum. The angles are haphazard, but somehow orderly. Green needle stalks slide into blue tips. They bulge from their limbs at the most peculiar angles, and some branches are missing clusters of them, but I sense an order to the arrangement. It is not too tall, but not too short either. The proportion of the base to the tip top is divine. And the cones. The cones! Greater harmony of craftsmanship I have never seen. Each bead of each cone's surface is like a little heart, each heart fused delicately to the next, but there exists a glorious symphony of the sizes as they march from large at the cone's equator to minute at its tip. Even the tiniest of them is immaculately cut.

"It's beautiful," I whisper.

"I don't like it," the boy says.

"Charlie!" Steward grabs his arm. "We talked about outbursts, and how Aesthete needs to do his job."

The boy shakes his head. "But mom!"

"No buts."

He crosses his arms, eyeing the splendid tree with revulsion plastered across his face. He wrenches his arm away from Steward's grasp and retreats until his back is up against the tree display across the aisle.

"Very sorry, Aesthete."

I wave it off. "I was a boy too once, you know."

"You seem quite fond of this one." She motions to the tree.

"I admit, there is something quite magnificently ordered to its chaos."

"I agree. But what do you make of that smell?"

I chuckle. "They have quite overdone the odor, haven't they? I suppose that is also part of its charm."

Steward shrugs. "It's just so pungent."

"The details in the cones, the proportions of... everything. All of it. See there! Even the partial decay of some needles and branches has been so scrupulously crafted. It is quite a work, isn't it?"

Steward looks back to her son, still scowling like a swine before this pearl of a conifer. His nose almost looks like a little snout—no. I retract such thoughts. They are cruel. I remind myself that his hatred is born of ignorance, and as he is Steward's son, he will receive the best education possible. Of ignorance, he will undoubtedly be absolved. Let him enjoy childish things today.

"Charlie," I say.

His scowl falls away as he turns his attention to me. Hesitantly, he walks a bit closer.

"A minus," I mutter to Steward, regarding the magnificent thing.

She raises an eyebrow.

"Just in case I happen to find something better."

She nods.

We walk and Charlie strides beside me.

"I want you to give the initial evaluation of the next tree, Charlie."

"Thank you, sir," he says.

I smile down at him.

We arrive before it.

"What do you think?" I say.

"Well, um." He rubs his hands around one another a few times. He gulps visibly. "It's um. The color's between blue and green. That seems pretty. And it's tall. Maybe a bit too tall? And the needles are kinda long. Maybe... um... G?"

I smile and nod. "That is a good first attempt."

Steward coughs and turns to cover her mouth.

I continue. "I'm glad you've caught the distinction regarding the coloration," I say. I pause to clear my scratchy throat. "And the height is an important note." I pause to cough. Steward is hacking louder now, doubled over. Even Charlie is coughing.

Red warning lights replace the dull white glow, and still we are all coughing, harder than ever. It is difficult to breathe.

White seeps in at the edges of my vision.

I fall.

My vision goes white.

I don't know how much time passes.

People around me, in suits. I am on a stretcher. I am in a bed. Machines beep.

"...terrestrial in nature..."

"...how'd they get it in there?"

"...passed the bioscans with a computer virus..."

"...bioorganic life from Earth. A simple tree..."

"...just like an art piece, the perfect ruse..."

I am weak, but I reach out, grab an arm. "No..." I hiss. My throat is dry and restricted.

"Whoa! Aesthete, sir, please stay calm!"

"No...!" I say again louder. The nurse's hand tries to set mine aside, back onto the soft mattress, but I grasp out at him anew through my fatigue.

"No," I insist. "Better than art."

Right and Proper

Mayor Davie Boro
Saila Township, Trini Province
Republic of Ukum

Dear Mayor Boro:

I am writing to inform you that I have been assigned to your Township's case, as we have yet to receive a response to the three automated notices issued to your office. You will find a detailed report of your Township's account attached to this message.

It is my duty at this time to inform you that, should your account remain in the red, the Igi will terminate energy distribution to your township at High Ashmin on

Mimin-Du.

Sincerely,
Su Kailey Verillo
Designation Ges-Limnu-Nis-Limmu
Igi Energy Corporation

—

Kailey tapped the large, rectangular button on her keyboard, and the holographic message before her folded over itself into the form of an envelope and flittered away. She pushed the window containing Saila Township's delinquency report down into her desk, closing it out.

With a quick swipe of her fingers, another delinquency report popped off the holographic stack at the corner of her desk and flew up to take the place of the former. This one detailed the overdue account for Woraya Township of Udinay Province. Judging from the stack, about half a dozen more remained.

She opened a new mail window and placed it beside the delinquency report. She had just placed her hands on the keyboard, when an itch worked its way up her spine. Recognizing the perturbation for what it was, she turned slowly to her right and stood, pushing her chair back—someone had entered her personal space.

Kailey found herself facing the tall and lanky Su Johann.

"How are you?" Johann asked.

Kailey nodded. "Well."

"Are those the delinquency reports?"

"They are."

His eyes lingered on the stack of holographic files. Kailey wondered as to whether or not she was being evaluated. It would have been odd, since she and Johann were near-peers.

Johann turned his attention back to her. "They need someone to run orientation today. Travis is out sick. If you're not too busy—?"

Kailey's eyes lit up. "I'll do it."

She knew better than to pass up an opportunity to take on more work, and it would reflect favorably upon her if even one of the recruits she trained went on to profit the company.

"Thanks," Johann said. Kailey noticed something in his eyes. He was relieved. Very odd. Had he been worried about taking the task on? If so, why? His efficiency rating was quite high; he could certainly handle the additional duty. She could think of no other reason he would pass on a career-enhancing assignment. His loss, she supposed.

Johann turned and disappeared into the sea shuffling Su. Holographic windows flittered in and out of existence atop wooden desks as Su darted between them, their grey and black business uniforms punctuating the white room, making the space seem a living static haze of people and desks against the walls.

Kailey leaned down and downloaded the orientation roster into her personal computer pad, grabbed it up, and unregistered her account from the desk. Her stack of delinquency reports fizzled away to nothing.

A Su she didn't recognize, a young man, rushed up to her. "Are you done here, Su...?"

"Kailey," she smiled. "Yes, I am."

He nodded his thanks, took a seat at the desk and registered his own account with it. A pile of holographic windows loaded, two stacks side by side, both piling up higher than his head.

No wonder he was in such a rush. Kailey wondered if his efficiency rating would allow him to remain a Su much longer. Not everyone was cut out for this kind of work.

Kailey wove through the sea of shuffling black suits, her heels clapping against the metal floor. She dodged other Su all around her, basking in the orderly chaos of commotion, the voices of her peers harmoniously asynchronous.

A grey metal rectangle zipped over the exit door of the office just as she approached it. It buzzed with a squealing sound, reminiscent of a long 'zrimmm,' which died away as it whisked past into the distance. Similar units ran across the walls of the service corridor Kailey passed into, the noise and bustle of chatting Su replaced with the comparatively quiet clomping of shoes against metal as multitudes of Igi workers of all ranks and stations traversed the halls.

Kailey veered toward the right wall instinctively as she joined the human foot traffic. She liked having other people to only a single side of her. Although she had to keep far enough away from the walls so as not to bump into the rectangles zipping past screaming zrim and zram. As a young recruit, she's gotten too near to the wall and let one career into her arm. She released a meager smile at the fond albeit ridiculous memory and shook her head to reinforce her stolid calm.

She glanced down at her computer and decided to review the orientation procedure intermittently as she walked. It was at least half a kilometer to the staging chamber. The rhythmic clomping of feet on metal and the intermittent announcements over the intercoms fell into the background of her perceptions as she swiped through documents that hovered in the air before her. She turned corners on reflex, letting muscle memory bring her closer to her destination.

She passed the large chambers for the tunnel shafts and the exothermic cores without realizing it. More announcements buzzed from the speakers, a staccato beat of meeting announcements and maintenance requests punctuated by the occasional personnel report.

A crackling tone erupted from the speakers, and Kailey lurched to a halt and dropped the computer to her side. Everyone in the halls, herself included, stared up at the nearest black, plastic-meshed speaker expectantly. A pang of dread stabbed her heart.

"Urgent update," the speaker voice said. "All Ningur to attention. Su Shaun, Designation Lipish Ninnu-Es... has a birthday celebration today. Stop by the lounge at limmu for cake, celery cubes, and juice." Kailey and everyone near her exhaled their fear. Such a tactless joke. And in the middle of work hours! A few scoffed at the speakers. All returned to their duties.

Kailey turned another corner, and her target came into view: the metal door to the staging chamber. She scanned her palm on the lock-panel, and the door slid open. Wincing and squinting, she strode into the brightly lit room, doing her best to force her facial muscles into something resembling normal despite the stabbing light.

The room itself was a garrulous mishmash of color, and the spongy carpeting felt wrong beneath her feat, not firm like the metal plating of the Igi-proper. This was all for the new recruits. Best to ease them in.

The room was surprisingly quiet. New recruits tended to be quite garrulous. Glancing around, Kailey realized the room was empty. Nearly empty—a lone woman stood against the wall beside the chamber's opposite exit, her hands clasped together in front of her. She had long brown hair and wore a pair of glasses. Her attire consisted of the kind of slacks and sweater that were popular with university students nowadays. The young woman straightened as Kailey drew nearer and tightened her grip on the tablet computer in her hands.

Kailey scanned the rest of the room. "Are you the only recruit today?"

"Yes, ma'am."

Unusual, but not unheard of. Also very inefficient. This was probably what had turned Johann off. Kailey turned on her heel, deciding to make the best of the situation.

"Follow me." Kailey led her toward the door, anxious to leave the glare. She nearly scanned her palm, but stopped herself. Recalling the proper procedure, she turned to the recruit. "What is your name?"

"Saga."

Kailey blinked a few times. An odd name, she thought, but decided to say nothing of it. "You may call me 'Su Ges-Limnu-Nis-Limmu.' It may take some time to learn the numerical nomenclature of the Igi. During your orientation, 'Su' will do. I encourage you to practice the full name tonight."

"Yes, ma'a— Su Ges-Limnu-Nis-Limmu."

Kailey retracted her hand from the door panel and turned to Saga yet again. "You are proficient with words?"

Saga responded with an imperious gaze, though not one quite of defiance, but rather the kind of stubborn nerve only young people these days were capable of.

"I have scored well in the linguistics," Saga said.

"I can see why you were selected. Those skills will be of some utility in the Igi."

Kailey opened the door, and the two of them stepped out into the grey halls, into the more familiar zrim and zram of the speeding rectangles and the hum of shuffling people. A wave of relief washed over Kailey. No more blaring light in her eyes or squishy floor beneath her feet.

"We'll begin immediately," Kailey announced. "This way, please."

Saga followed in her wake. Whenever Kailey looked back to make sure she was still there, Saga would have her head turned toward some portal, some person, some passing mech, with the most wondrous, naïve light in her eyes. She quickly turned her gaze back to Kailey on such occasions.

After many minutes of narrowing and darkening halls, Kailey brought Saga to the door of the energy refinery, a massive chamber at the edge of the Igi facility.

Kailey scanned her hand against the pitch black door panel, and it slid open.

"Su Ges-Limnu-Nis-Limmu?"

"Yes?" Kailey turned to her. She was barely visible in

the low light.

"I have questions. When might I—?"

"You will be assigned a computer and a number of digital and holographic books. Should those not answer your questions, you may submit a request for further reference material to the Zuüm. That is a the Igi's—" She hesitated, recalling the word used for such places above. "—library."

Saga nodded, and Kailey led her inside. A soft white glow suffused the space, wrapping around them. Her eyes, accustomed to such changes, adjusted rapidly.

"This," Kailey said, "is the energy refinery."

She turned to see how Saga had adjusted to the lighting, and was surprised to see her drawing her hands up to her face. Tears glistened at the edges of Saga's eyes. Kailey watched this, feeling the vague murmur of unease build into something more aghast. Displays of intense emotion in the Igi...? How utterly uncouth.

"Is something wrong?" Kailey asked.

"Oh, Su Ges-Limnu-Nis-Limmu... it's extraordinary."

Kailey glanced out at the conveyors and pulleys and cranes, the long rows of shiny, transparent-grey tungsten polyhedrons, each being drilled and pricked and prodded by the refinery's machines. Blots of nanite haze suffused their surfaces as they trundled about the room atop plasticine belts.

It all felt very orderly. Very usual.

Saga gulped, swallowing a small yelp, nearly causing Kailey to jump.

"What is it, Miss Saga?" Kailey demanded.

"Oh, these things here..."

"The lattices?"

"Yes..." She walked up to the nearest conveyor, shuddering and putting on an awful show. Ud workers gawked at her until Kailey shot her gaze at them, at which point they did their best to ignore the pair of them and get on with their work.

"Miss Saga." Kailey frowned. "I should remind you that assignment to the Igi is a position that one should afford a degree of respect."

"That one there." Saga pointed to a dodecahedron structure composed of twisting lattices and spiral formations.

"What about it?"

"It's beautiful. So many of them are beautiful."

"They are merely transparent tungsten lattices formed from the fractal complexity of objects in other universes."

"No," Saga said. "They're more than that."

Shock rippled through Kailey, wracking every nerve she possessed and shooting her up with a narcotic hit of indignation, a splash of anger right on its tail. "Whatever do you mean, 'no'?"

"Many are beautiful, but this one... Words fail me. To say it is magnificent is to do it an injustice." She walked up to the dodecahedron just as the wheels of the conveyor spun, pushing all the polyhedrons forward a meter. Saga merely sidestepped to remain standing before her selection. "See how it's ordered near the center? The interior is a simple lattice, but it grows more angles and curves as you go outward, until the edges, with those helixes and spirals. Oh, Su Ges-Limnu-Nis-Limmu. It's amazing."

The hunk of transparent tungsten remained to Kailey nothing more than a hunk of transparent tungsten, despite the recruit's description.

"I know they become power," Saga said. "How is that exactly?"

"Quantum decoherence."

"Ah." The syllable fell with resounding melancholy. "We remove them from all-possibility."

"Yes. That is how power is generated." Kailey clamped her lips shut, sealing back a huff of exasperation. Saga would get no glowing recommendation from her. In fact, she would recommend the recruit look for other work at the end of this 'orientation.' Less than an hour in, and already Kailey could guess at the reason Johann's smug reticence—he had already heard from someone on the outside about this young woman and had successfully pawned off this waste of time. Perhaps even Travis was sitting in his quarters doing real work, only pretending to be ill.

However, the matter of Saga's orientation was not a duty that Kailey could slough off. There were procedures to follow, and Kailey would abide them.

She was good at that.

Kailey showed Saga about the refinery, keeping her explanation of the decoherence process going at such a clip as to give Saga no time to ask any more questions, and also as to avoid witnessing the recruit's emotions displayed bare upon her childish face, a little showcase for all of the Ud workers in the refinery to see. Saga would look up at Kailey expectantly every so often, clearly desirous to ask a question, but Kailey gave her no opportunity, continuing through the standard explanation and into the complexities of the quantum decoherence process.

She took Saga through the whole day in a similar fashion, from the energy refinery to the arsenal to the shield grid to the Zuüm, and finally to the laboratories. When Kailey's voice grew hoarse from talking, Saga even had the nerve to ask if she could get her superior some water. 'Getting' indeed! How quaint.

Kailey produced her computer, and instructed the nanite control system to synthesize a glass of water into her hand. That prompted a lesson in basic nanorobotic architecture and the licensing procedures that would be part of Saga's ramp-up. Until then she was to use the pre-programmed synthesis chambers in the commons. Not that she would be training here very long.

The deference and quiet attention she'd demonstrated since her outburst in the refinery was not fooling Kailey. 'Beauty.' How absurd.

Kailey dropped Saga off in the Yuüm, in one of the recruit hallways that probably contained her new quarters. Kailey then made some excuse about needing to prepare for the next day's duties, and retreated deeper into the Yuüm toward the halls of the Su.

As she walked, she passed a few of her Su peers whom she had met on various assignments, and with each she exchanged a curt nod, a welcome reprieve after enduring hours of Saga's emotional exuberance.

Kailey reached her quarters, and the door slid open with a light rumble just as an announcement sputtered from the speaker set into the ceiling.

Her quarters were dark, just the right amount of ambient light. She kept few possessions. A desk, table, and bed stood out starkly, protruding from the blank walls.

An empty shelf was set into the metal walls above the bed. A small pile of technical manuals lay on the floor near the door to the bathroom.

Kailey strode directly to her desk, made herself comfortable in the chair, paying careful attention to her posture, and registered her account. With a flick of the wrist and tap of a holographic menu item, an evaluation form shimmered into view before her.

An hour's worth of typing later, Kailey had drafted and edited her recommendation to the Eshlu that Saga's internship be terminated immediately. The young woman would be reviewed, of course, by at least two other Su, but Kailey held no doubt that her peers would arrive at the same conclusion she had: Saga was unfit to accomplish any of the necessary tasks within the Igi.

What were they teaching young people in the colleges these days?

Kailey moved her outstretched finger toward the send button on the holographic interface and found herself holding it in midair.

What was the matter? She asked herself that question mentally many times, not quite believing her own intuition. But there it was. She could not ignore it. You don't become a high-ranking Su without understanding yourself. Mastering self-knowledge was crucial, and Kailey could neither shake nor ignore the feeling that something was—

Off.

She stood, exited.

The zrim zram of the rectangles across the walls seemed miles away as her shoes clopped down the metal hallway. Her heart pounded. She was perspiring as she walked, which made her walk faster (to minimize the problem of being seen in such a state), but that only increased her mounting anxiety—such a terrible feedback loop!

She practiced her breathing techniques and focused her mind on the path out of the Yuüm and toward the energy refinery. She made a map of the halls in her head and focused on that with all her mental fortitude.

After a seemingly endless blur of hallways, she found herself in the dark hallway standing before the energy refinery door. She scanned her hand and entered.

The room was the same as before, wasn't it? All whirring and grinding and the trundling of conveyors and the hums and hushed vibrato of busy nanite clusters.

"Excuse me," Kailey said to one of the late-shift Ud workers, who wore the red helmet and dark visor and crimson jumpsuit of her caste. "I was here this morning, around ussu. This conveyor here was full of lattices. Have those been decohered yet?"

The Ud woman shook her head and led Kailey toward the back of the room, to a place where all the various conveyors converged into a single line. At its end, the tungsten lattices passed into a dark tunnel, though a faint glow emanated from deep within, shrouding the encroaching lattices in a dim, white light.

"These were probably near the door around ussu."

"Thank you," Kailey said, her eyes already scanning them over. Aha! There it was, the lattice that had taxed Saga's emotions so. Kailey walked up to it.

"Will that be all?" Had she not spoken, Kailey would

not have noticed the Ud's presence.

"Yes." Kailey's eyes remained fixed on the lattice. "Thank you. That will be all."

What had Saga seen in this? Yes, the form was regular in the center and grew more chaotic at the edges. But it was just a lattice. Wasn't it? Nothing to get excited about. No need for excessive emotion.

Kailey pulled up her tablet computer and scanned the lattice. Its composition was the mathematical expression of an object from another universe, some artefact that Igi nanites had surveyed and analyzed. Their record of the object's signature had been used to construct the lattice. When the lattice was decohered, the thing it represented would be erased from all of possibility across all of quantum space-time. But the energy, oh the energy they derived from such events! That made it all worthwhile.

What would this lattice obliterate within the hour?

The data populated upon her computer's display: Quantum plane identification hash: 7ae9bfb239d0, artefact number: Shar-Gesh-U-Min-Nimin-Nish, name: "The Twelfth Night", originator: "William Shakespeare".

Kailey sounded out the bizarre syllables comprising the lattice's name and originator, the wholly unctuous combinations of consonants and vowels.

She cringed, and a foul taste filled her mouth.

If this was 'beauty,' Kailey would happily embrace crudity. The thing correlating to this hunk of tungsten, whatever it was, would indeed be better off utilized as a forcefield, reactor coolant, a computer part, or... a glass of water! Something practical.

It was decided. She would send her recommendation. How comical that she had come so close to self-doubt! She decided, as she turned on her heel, that she must better control her emotions and not let aberrant recruits muddy her perceptions of right and proper things.

Kailey looked over her shoulder, took one final glance at the lattice as it neared the dark chasm, then strode out of the refinery wearing a satisfied, confident grin.

| EVERYTHING AND NOTHING |

∞

Binary

Zero to one.

A vibrant fluctuation from nothing to something.

The void ripples and distends, a blinding
plasma, showering down vigor, calamity, awe, terror.

Pinpricks appear, black and dark against the inferno. The great mass of intensity coalesces into vibrato pools, washing out the black with its catastrophic churning.

But the pockets of void persist, returning again and again. The destruction dances blissfully onward, swirling amongst itself, elegiac, a dance of ecstasy, bursting with power and enormity of space-time all compacted and screaming at the margins into ever more of itself, all swallowed up in writhing, twirling, consuming coruscation. Existence performs a virtuoso riot.

Swells of activity converge, smashing and grinding into one another with incredible force. The ebb and flow courses into cosmic currents, and the energy collapses into enormous cataclysms of outstanding power, that pull everything around them into gravitational calamities, roaring and screaming. A brief flicker of small but tremendous complexity, there and gone again. The loci of the ebb and flow swell, but so do the places of nothing in between. Space distends, and the fire burns bright, but ever faster does the naught expand between them. The riot dims to a mere swell of power and bluster, frightened and retreating.

The remaining pockets of grand activity cluster together, huddling as the enormity of nothing surrounds them, no longer tiny dots to be washed away, but enormous, dark voids. They grow more distant from one another by the moment, the light of their brethren fading. They draw inward upon themselves in a vast illusion of maintaining the status quo under the pressure of dwindling resources.

Many collapse, losing all their brilliance, and become dim husks of their former glory. Or worse, they invert upon themselves into demons of distended space-time, terrorizing all about them to nil.

Awe wanes into a solipsism of calm, the tiny dots rippling away into bits of glory that blare tinily against the spreading stillness.

A flickering, hissing out to nothing, small and weak.

One to zero.

Production Dates

Thinking Machines
Ghost Daemons   October 23, 2014
Adaptive   July 17, 2014

Weird Pets
Felis Catus   June 5, 2014
Fair Trade   October 9, 2014
Xenosociology   June 11, 2015

The Coding Life
A Programmer's Tale   August 28, 2014
Rune-Driven Spellcraft   May 14, 2015

The *Introduction*, and the section introductions to *Thinking Machines*, *Weird Pets*, and *The Coding Life* were initially drafted on January 15, 2017. The section introductions to *Troubled Relationships*, *Chaos and Fear*, *Society*, *Aesthetic*, and *Everything and Nothing* were drafted on January 16, 2017. All these sections were revised on January 15-16, 2019.

www.ingramcontent.com/pod-product-compliance
Lightning Source LLC
Chambersburg PA
CBHW030323200626
46816CB00006BA/1902